DJ *WAGs*
HOUSEWIVES
OF HOUSE

by
Jaqi Loye-Brown

MT
Ink

MT-Ink.co.uk

First published by MT Ink in 2018

© Jaqi Loye-Brown

ISBN: 978-1-9164784-1-1

Cover design: MT Ink
Stylist: Reena Qureshi

Jaqi Loye-Brown asserts the moral right to be
identified as the author of this work

Writing is not a form of "art for art's sake" but a tool to decode social relations - Roland Barthes

Contents

Jaqi Loye-Brown

Brainstorm In A Teacup

Croissants and Danishes stuck to the doilies in the centre of the beech wood table. The coffee and tea spillages told a story of their own during the three-hour, drawn out meeting, Charlotte was leading. No one could agree with the direction following the pilot viewing earlier that morning.

"So what do you all make of the rough edits so far? Is Gillian coming?" enquired Polly.

"Yes, sorry she's on her way," replied Dorrit. "She snuck out the viewing to take a call. She said to start without her for now."

"Let's just go round the room," continued Charlotte. "I need everybody's input, but I'm sure we all agree that this could become quite a controversial show. Do we go down the sensationalist route …or tone it down? Thoughts please."

The TV production team – senior producers Edna Wright and Dorrit Saunders, senior reality director Charlotte Green, assistant producer Polly Schraber and the casting producer Laura Cave – were gathered in the West Kensington office meeting room at noon. For September the weather was still fine, warmer than August.

There was a silence. No one wanted to go first. So Charlotte prompted them.

"Okay. Let me put it this way. The concept of

7

housewives is already a well-worn theme, but will these ladies appeal to the same audience? Are they too old? I mean DJ WAGs is an original take on it, but would younger WAGs appeal to a younger audience?"

Edna stood up for her protégés.

"They are the rave generation in middle age. That audience is already there. Pretty much everyone in that age group and older were clubbing or partying in fields. Even if they weren't, they knew people who had. The Acid House generation was one some felt they had missed out on. But, historically it did change the face of clubbing as we know it. I believe there is an appetite for something like this. If we're not careful we could be failing our audience by stereotyping our female watchers. They are so much more sophisticated with a relevant social life. Many of whom still go out raving. Some with their grown-up children even! Come on...we've all had our moments...even now? Admit it...it is a thing!"

"Yes, but do they want to see grown women bang on the gear, especially as parents?" reasoned Laura. "What kind of a picture does that paint?"

"Authenticity is the key word here. Isn't that what we stand for, authentic reality?" reasoned Edna. "By keeping it real, yes, it may be controversial, but it is 'real life'. They are successful women, running their homes and raising their kids, doing all the things expected of them but they also play hard. Why should they not play as hard as their male counterparts? I mean they even call themselves 'Five-Go-Hard'."

"Hmmm? The drugs element could affect the commercial aspect. We really have to think about that."

"But surely that's the edge, though? This show could turn the genre on its head."

At that point Gillian Morris-Quaid swung in wearing

a very loud Vivienne Westwood coat.

"I agree, the druggy aspect concerns me," said Gillian, quickly picking up the theme. "Let's get Business Affairs in. Can someone call Marcus? Get him to come down here, a-sap," she added, gesticulating to no one in particular.

The intern Emilee, burst in holding the door behind her. "Shall I order some more refreshments? Gillian, can I get you anything?" she asked feebly.

"Actually, a double soya macchiato, from the nice place. Please."

"Right!"

"Charlotte, update me darling."

"Well, according to Laura the faces don't gel together enough," explained Charlotte. "She thinks the idea works well enough, but the onscreen chemistry is off. She can't see it. And Polly feels the same. Dorrit thinks if we saw more of the men that would ground the show in terms of it being about the lifestyle of DJs and how it affects their partners. From what I saw, it could be edited one of two ways. Either could work. As is, it lacks direction. I think we should choose one and run with it. Go sensational with it. Or play safe in terms of commercialism..."

"Let me interrupt you there, darling," said Gillian. "I thought it was bloody good telly, to be honest. I just loved it! It's very raw, but that's exactly what I found appealing. It's different...therefore fresh. Tell you what I'd like to do. Let me shop it around for now. I have a talk at The Guild. Let me get some feedback from a few people. I think we do have something here. But I stress, the druggy element is questionable. Then again, that's what I quite liked, haha..."

Six Months Earlier

The problem with Piper Blair, at 38, the youngest of the Five-Go-Hard, was that she could make a new 'best-friend-forever' before breakfast. A triumph if 'forever' meant lasting past teatime. TV-Edna was the latest such acquaintance.

Piper was a social media blogger, proud and loud about it. She had a little sister relationship with Dande, ten years her senior, who regularly lectured her ..."for her own good"... about the many social faux pas Piper instigated.

It seemed Piper was forever introducing random after random 'persons of interest', to Dande and the group. It never quite clicked.

This time, however, the girl done good.

Edna Wright was a freelance series producer, single and ambitious, living in a shared house in West Hampstead. She had savings to put down a deposit on a Peckham flat, in south London, but wasn't convinced she could live there yet. She had to make a decision soon as the prices were increasing, even in 'da Sarf'.

The Five-Go-Hard had been meeting up regularly with newbie Edna at a tapas restaurant on Portobello Road, the Golborne Road end. They enjoyed her insider tales of the celebrity world and this time conversation turned to the scandals in TV reality shows. Were they real or set up?

The debate had begun in earnest.

"Tell you what, bet we've got some stories. Not sure you could broadcast any of it, though," cackled Dande, before adding: "Oh my God! We'd be like The Housewives of House!"

"Too funny! Housewives of House...OMG! Can you imagine us lot on the telly?" jumped in Nancy.

"Yeah, haha, Housewives of House Music All Night Long! Say whaaat?" sang Clara.

"The time it takes you to put your makeup on they'd be showing the repeats!"

"Oi!"

With the girls suitably inebriated, Edna noticed how quickly the banter took off.

"She's got a point, Nance. Remember 'Beefa, Clara...when we did three freaking parties and she was still applying bronzer by the time we'd got back?"

"Yeah, you was clueless! Nance, you were like, 'any of you got a spare mascara brush?'"

"You didn't even get into two of them clubs...ya' fuckers..."

Clara Molehill, the original party animal of the group, had been the brunt of the stories a thousand times. But it was Nancy's turn to take a bashing. They always took it in good humour.

"Clara, what about you? When you got so paranoid you locked yourself and Flemming in that hotel room, remember? He missed his set?"

Dande joined in.

"Two grand that cost him, didn't it?"

Suki didn't want to be left out. "And the rest!"

Piper and the gang wailed in hysterics. Anything that put their overinflated ego-driven-DJ partners in their place was fair game.

Edna enjoyed watching the mirth bubble over as

11

it developed, but she could also see the pound signs flashing before her with every glint of her recently fitted veneers.

Was she witnessing the next big thing in reality TV?

These west London ladies were bohemian chic, with their contemporary outlook and hedonistic lifestyle. Their world was not as 'obvious' nor garish as football WAGs, nor were they as obnoxious as the obscenely wealthy Amercian WAGs.

They definitely had potential cross-over mass appeal to the young and older age groups because of their superstar DJ partners, the music element and their über-glam Ibizan connections. Win-win.

"Hey girls...it's actually not that bad of an idea." broached Edna gently.

"My idea! My idea!" claimed Dande.

The waiter came round to tidy up the sticky mess the girls had made with their Limoncello shots.

"I mean it, guys." Edna's voice took on a professional air, "We're always on the look out for new concepts or re-working old ones. Would you be up for something like that? You are all a little edgy and kind of cool - in a very classy way, of course."

The friends glanced at each other for mutual approval. A nervous hush descended before Dande took control of the situation.

"Are you serious? If you're serious, Edna?" she appealed.

"Well...yes. The best ideas come about just like this. But I would have to run it past a few people first. Let me whisper around. I mean, you never know."

"How soon could you find out?" Suki, often coming and going from Hong Kong, for work, but mostly shopping, was thinking about her own commitment to something like this.

"It's ever so involved. What I do is, pitch the idea to the 'Concept & Development' team of the production company I work for and we try and get format clearance and potential commissioners onboard. There are so many ways we could spin it. The first thing is whether my exec-producer will consider it and perhaps shoot a pilot. I mean, this could be two, three or more years in the making. Although there are exceptions."

Edna foresaw the headache ahead of her and wished she hadn't said anything so soon. She had got too relaxed in their company.

"Wowzas!" Dande was smitten with the possibilities. "We could be in our own series? Think of the sponsorship deals, guys? Edna. Please look into it for us. Please. We are so up for it. I've been waiting for this for…well, all my life, really."

"No pressure then? Hahaha. Leave it with me. Let me get the bill."

Edna scurried to scoop the enclosed receipt before any of the others could grab it.

They were all heading back to Dande's for a night cap, with a view to a cheeky school night sesh, with a bump of mud here, a line there and a spliff. Usually, after any indulgence, Suki was the one who stepped in to round up the kids for school on those 'morning afters'. The best 'auntie' ever, especially as she was a lightweight drinker, thus generally the most sober… most of the time.

Outside the restaurant, while they waited for an Uber SUV, Edna made her excuses and promised to hang out longer next time.

Earlier That Day

"Did anyone see you?" Eli probed in horror.

He leaned in for a kiss, holding Piper close, her Porsche Cayenne's armrest and console allowing, and continued to kiss the teardrops over her lashes.

"Hmmm? Salty...yum".

"Stop it you weirdo!"

The light relief melted away the angst.

"Charlie said you was back. You haven't replied to any of my texts for ages now. I haven't had any sleep!"

The bronzed, mighty Mauritian brute tried to tickle her under her bust.

"Get lost! Stop it, Eli. Stop!"

But under his gaze she knew she was not going to get him to make sense of anything.

The lover's tryst was as arduous and passionate as their first embrace in 2008. They knew each other's weaknesses and whenever one waned, the other would pick things right back up from where they had left off.

Hidden behind the steamed windows, they sat up. It was time for a proper chat.

"Babe, I can't bear it," begged Piper.

Add Friend

Dande had met DJ Eli Stefano on the Eurostar to Paris. She was hanging with a hen party when he boldly walked up to her in front of them and asked-whether she was single. He invited her to come watch him play. She had mistakenly thought he was a musician or sportsman. Apart from his caramel glow she was taken by his bravado. A load of drunken women on the lash didn't scare him and she a big bird too. Huge points for effort.

Fourteen odd years in, she was lumbered - the only one in the group still unmarried.

"I'm a mug," she would often say to him. "You must have seen me coming."

To which he would lovingly reply: "We can all see you coming!"

She found him poking fun at her 5'10 height endearing. He was a warm character. Gregarious and charismatic, the life and soul of...

It was almost as if he had latched on to DJing as a crutch for excessive clubbing. Unfortunately, this charm turned to smarm with the fanbase of women he often attended to personally, earning him the nickname Eli-Down-With-Anyone.

Yet, he and Dande, on the face of it, appeared to be a tight couple.

When they went out clubbing, partying, at festivals or concerts, he only had eyes for her. At home he was truly devoted. He just wasn't there as often as she would like. But as soon as her back was turned, any woman with a smile on legs rendered him powerless to resist temptation. He lapped up every bit of attention he received.

Dande existed in Eli's world without the slightest idea of the dog that he was. He adored her devotion to his son. He had got his ex, Amy pregnant after a drunken one-off sex session shortly after dating Dande.

By the time he and Dande had made it official several months later, the baby was born. She fell in love with and immediately accepted baby Bertram, who they nicknamed Bertie. Amy was in no fit state to bring him up. It was decided between Eli and Amy's haughty ex-actress mother Claudia Flint-Dunn, that Eli was awarded sole custody. Dande was fast-tracked into parenthood before their relationship had bedded in.

*****

DJ Charlie Fenchurch was at the top of his game. Mix compilations, sell out gigs at every festival...Ibiza royalty...all round legend. Tall, dark and blandsome. His status was his beauty. He met the petite Piper poolside. Where else? Ibiza. She had become stuck to a sunbed, entangled by her extensions and neck-lace. Several people came to her rescue, including Dande and Eli, whom she hadn't yet befriended.

Her eyes met Charlie. For him it was love at first sight. But for Piper that was nothing new. She was still in a relationship with an entertainment lawyer who was at the bar when all the commotion took place. Dande was making it all about herself, laughing and bantering the attention away from the svelte beauty upstaging her.

Piper had been caught steadfastly and had to be cut free. Charlie was the first to dash off and fetch 'a tool' from his rucksack. Her tanned skin was glistening and intensely bronzed. She smelled of an expensive scent. He was well and truly taken in by her.

"Here he comes! Charlie to the rescue!" Dande was quick to spot.

As the banter continued a small crowd gathered.

Charlie fiddled with the small silver DJ torch in his hand. One twist revealed a Swiss Army knife-like multi-functioning tool hidden inside. It had passed through countless airport security checks undetected.

"This little gem has got me out of all sorts..." he reported with a strain as he tugged at the stubborn knots.

"You lucky girlie! Superstar DJ saves the day!"

It was at this comment, that Piper suddenly paid more attention to the 'tall and bland' man in the nautical Tommy Hilfiger swimmers.

She stared for a moment, enough to recognise him, looking so very different from his publicity shots. She smiled at him from her awkward position with a grateful nod. It was to be the first encounter of many that were to follow.

When he eventually got around to asking her out, she had only been split from her lawyer ex-boyfriend a week!

Matchmaking credits to her new bestie, Dande. Charlie and Eli were mates anyway, so the girls had spent the rest of that fateful holiday joined at the hip almost.

Eventually Piper moved into Charlie's Westbourne Park townhouse, down the road from Dande and Eli's in Queens Park. A couple of years later she became the fabulous wife of superstar DJ Charlie Fenchurch, the envy of many a DJ WAGs: Housewives of House. Dande was her Maid of Honour.

It was only after her wedding party that she got to know Clara, Nancy and Suki, whose DJing husbands, Flemming, Baxta and Razr respectively, were close friends of Charlie's on the clubbing circuit. Dande took over and her house became the regular meeting point for the ladies.

It took WhatsApp to arrive for them to establish the name 'Five-Go-Hard'.

Dande Lyon's For Queen's Park

The open planned kitchen and Moroccan themed conservatory in Dande's Queen's Park mansion terrace near the park was a decent party space for those in the know.

Dande would organise 'DJ widow' nights for the ladies when their 'boys' played out over evenings and weekends...Especially so from June through October when the dreaded Ibiza opening to closing residencies took over on one of the most hedonistic and beautiful islands in Europe. With it came the pressure of gorgeous 'fresh young tings' vying for their boys' attention, lining up in their skimpy frippery in a bid to bag one DJ for life. If there was ever such a thing!

They were undeniably threatened by the 'open' hunting season for their DJ partners. Holding their nerve was a mission that came with the territory.

"I love the way you've decorated your home, Dande," gushed Edna. "Lived here long?"

"Yes, back when it wasn't so popular. I love the Moorish influence when it comes to interiors. Always have."

"Have you seen the conservatory Edna? You should see it before you leave. It's like looking at the stars at night from a North African Bedouin tent."

Piper was buttering up TV-Edna as usual.

Building trust was an essential part of the job for

Edna. She knew she was being accepted into the fold whenever she was invited out, but this was her first visit to Dande's and for good reason. After a few months, the order came from on high to deliver the news they had held their breaths for.

She had the information the Five-Go-Hard were all desperately trying not to appear too keen about. Everybody wants to be on telly, don't they?

Aware that the atmosphere was feeling a little too staid for Dande's liking, she ushered everyone from the double reception room into the kitchen to get the bubbly out and sit in her conservatory. At floor level, sitting on the off-white Berber rugs and cushions and pouffes there could only be good news, she assumed. The 'wows' abounded at her latest Moroccan lamp. Edna leading the praise stopped short.

"Your taste is impeccable, Dande. Look forward to filming it soon, as you're all gonna be on the telly! They've agreed to shoot a pilot!"

The bubbly went everywhere. For once Dande did not care. Piper shrieked and Clara whooped while the rest echoed each other.

Nothing else out of Edna's mouth made sense as the Five-Go-Hard were on the verge of going extra hard. When the tequila and samba shots came out, so did the gear, all over Dande's kitchen island as they got to their feet to celebrate.

Not wishing to party-poop, Edna was mindful not to alienate her new friends-cum-talent when turning down a line of coke and other Class As. As a result, she ended up drinking way more sambucas than usual to compensate. She did pause for concern at their disregard for getting on it in her presence.

There was a point when every single one of the ladies had collared her in different corners of the house, off their faces, in her face, for a quick, brief, quiet "chat about things".

The hastily ordered Uber taxi had arrived when she said her goodbyes. Clara saw her to the door, mobile-in-hand, walking up the pathway, looking for someone in another car up the road.

"Mind how you go Edna! Thanks for everything again!" whispered Clara loudly. It was the early hours. Waving her off, it was only seconds later that a Mini Clubman pulled up with two blonde female friends.

"Myrtle, darling…how was the party?" Clara spoke into the wound-down passenger side window.

"It was a good night. It was still going on when we left. You remember Liberty?"

"Hi Liberty, long time! Send my love to Freddy."

"Listen it's cold, hun. Have you got?"

"I don't come out for just the one, Clara, but as it's you. Hahaha!"

"Dande called it on again. We're celebrating, but my lips are sealed."

"Oh yes? You're not preggers?"

"Naah! Give over!"

"Yeah, sorry, Clar…pay me later…"

"Nice one darling, mwah!" Clara quickly tucked the wrap in her pocket.

Dande came to see why her door was still open and caught Clara sneaking back inside.

"Was that Myrtle? She still serving up?"

"Yes, just got us some extra doodah…we gonna be on telly! Whoohoo!"

Dande And Delivered

Traipsing around the house in crimson, be-jewelled Moroccan slippers, Dande was getting more intensely annoyed. As he got prepped for the opening parties, Eli was making their home life all about him again. Over-whelmed with her responsibilities, she was aggrieved by control issues that made domesticity seem easy. She had two kids to look after: Eli's teenage son Bertie and her six-year-old daughter, Lola who, by comparison, was a sweetheart...no trouble at all.

Bertie was a handful. She was his mummy while his real mother was circumnavigating the revolving rehab door. He was becoming aware about the addictions that caused his abandonment. His father Eli wasn't around enough to ask him about it and he was also wary of being disloyal to his step-Mummy.

It was a big job for Dande to take on when, she herself, had her own addiction issues. Okay, she was a functioning alcoholic, like so many of her partying peers. She could handle her shit. This area with its white powder trail, stream of wine, shots and gin cocktails was somewhere you could lose days of the week; you were under the radar of the Kensal Triangle. Unlike Bermuda, no mystery to solve there.

She had joined Alcoholics Anonymous, and also Nar-cotics sibling , but mostly attended their sister Al-Anon sessions initially to keep informed on how best to help her stepson come to terms with his real mother's addictions. However, as a result, she unexpectedly found herself facing a few demons of her own. She deeply resented Eli for causing her to face these issues head on so prematurely in her life.

But Dande's bond with Eli seemed unbreakable and she knew this was the glue that kept her relationship with Eli on track. But it was she who did all the work…hands on.

"What delivery?" yelled Dande down the receiver.

"I forgot, just got a text. Sign for it will ya, please…?"

"What is it and how long have I got to wait in…for fucks sake, E!"

"New flight cases, care of the sponsors, babe. Fucking vinyl's back, honey. Don't blame me for that!" smirked Eli.

"Seriously, this is gonna fuck up my day big time. I told you, the TV people want to see us this afternoon before the shoot tomorrow. I've got no idea what time we'll finish so need to sort some things out before the childminder gets here. Bertie is acting up! He's been chucked out of school again and reckons he's too old for a babysitter. I don't need this today. I don't have a clue what to wear and won't have time to fit in the hairdressers. They're filming us tomorrow…bloody hell, Eli! Why aren't you here, helping me out!"

"Stop shouting, will you? My ears can't take anymore. I have to get this mix down by tonight. I fly out a couple of days. This mix is phat! Wanna hear?"

"What? While you play at records I've got to cancel stuff so I can stay in and wait for the postman? Piss taker!"

"Okay, okay, I'll let you know if I can get back earlier. I want to help."

"That's all I'm asking, babe. You know how much I want this."

"Completely. I'm backing you all the way, baby."

"That's all I want…your support," whined Dande. "I just need this something for me, you know?"

"Love ya, hun. Good luck! Knock 'em dead. Gotta go!"

The Pilot

It was an early start. The Five-Go-Hard were hyper after two cars were sent to pick them up. Such an exciting day.

Suki had volunteered to do a style makeover on Clara and Nancy. One car would pick them up from hers. It was only fair because Dande had secretly insisted on bringing a local stylist mate of theirs, Reena Qureshi to maintain quality control on the production's designated costume people. Dande was not going to appear on TV wearing high street. She was going to text the address to Reena once there. They were all being taken to a secret location just outside London. The second car would pick up Dande and Piper.

They gawped at the beautifully-coiffed grounds at the pile in Totteridge. It wasn't long before the giant fuss began with a melee of costume stylists and make-up artists, while other production team and crew members made demands on who was to do what, to whom, where and when.

Suki needn't have bothered with a style makeover on the girls after all. There was a room full of rails and trestle table with a cornucopia of accessories and footwear; a treasure trove of designer garments that had the squealing ladies enthralled.

"Oh nooo, I love these, but they don't fit!" groaned Dande, hogging the shoe area. "Hang on, oh,

I like these ones too!"

"Hey gimme those! What size are these?" Clara was straight in to try a pair of Stella McCartney heels, immediately alerting the attention of all the ladies, desperate for the same shoe to fit them. They were hyped and making a real racket until the official stylist, Sofia Sieben stepped in.

"Okay guys...ladies, ladies...settle down now. Sorry. Okay. Listen my name is Sofia Sieben and I am here to help you choose a look for yourselves today. We have put together a variety of garments based on the measurements and suggestions you supplied. Can I ask you all to get two or three options from each of the rails. This is Georgio and Lucy, my assistants. They will help you. Bring your choices over to them when you've done. Don't worry about accessories for now. Shoes and handbags will be provided afterwards. We've been lent some luxe items we're sure you're going to love! More to come on that later! Right, sort yourselves out then. Ten more minutes..."

After the calm of listening, the hype returned in earnest.

The Five-Go-Hard were united by their common social interests because of their DJ partners, but their styles were very different. As the years went by there were overlaps of each other's influences, especially with holiday clothes. They made special shopping trips to Selfridges, Bond Street and Harvey Nichols. When it came to the High Street, it had to be Hobbs, Cos, Jigsaw, Whistles, All Saints and sometimes Kooples. But they shopped online from Net-a-Porter, Matches Fashion, Acne Studios and Browns. Living where they did, so close to Portobello Road they also supported local boutiques and ransacked vintage and thrift shops for their trade mark quintessential style.

Emilee popped her head around the door as the ladies, now dressed in their new garms, were zipping up or tucking in.

"Hey guys! You all look amazing!" she clapped. "Can we have three of you for makeup now. Follow me please."

"I'll go after...just gotta make a quick call," exclaimed Piper hurriedly.

"Shall I wait for you?" wondered Dande as she texted Reena for her whereabouts.

"No, no, no ...you go ahead. Just a few things to sort out. You look hot, mamma!"

"Thank you. It's Chlöe."

Piper ran down the staircase, through the open hallway, hurriedly passed curious film crew and their paraphernalia, via the greenhouse conservatory, out into the expansive gardens. She eventually found a privacy-friendly privet hedge to make her call in peace.

"Hi, darling, just thought I'd make a sneaky call and talk to you quickly."

"Piper?! How's the shoot going then? Haven't even heard from Dande yet. She must be in her element."

Eli's mirth soon curtailed.

"I didn't call you to talk about her! Babe, I'm just missing you, that's all. I want to see you before you go."

"Babe, we're cutting it close. You know how hard this is. If you can't do it anymore just say. We can stop."

"Why do you always say that? Can't I say I miss you, when I do?"

"I miss you too Sweetie Pi...I just get nervous when...when...when you're with Dande. If she ever finds out…"

"I'm outside, in the gardens, there's no-one about."

"Even so, babe. Look, I can't talk now. I've got a package to collect and stuff. Is this 'cos I'm leaving for Ibiza tomorrow? I will call you, you know. Love ya!"

"I want to say goodbye properly…love you back," sulked Piper.

Upstairs were her beautifully coiffed friends, the almost unrecognisable DJ WAGs. Nancy was in Burberry, Suki opted for Christopher Kane and Clara went for a colourful Mary Katranzou dress. Dande had totally underestimated the costume team. It was awkward when Reena arrived. She approved the looks and interfered with their accessory choices. Behind the scenes an incensed Sofia had some harsh words to say about it to the production team.

Piper was dragged hurriedly into makeup.

"OMG! You guys look the fucking nuts!" said Piper, cricking her neck looking back.

"Where were you? Everyone's been looking."

"Dande, that lippy is to die for! What did they do in there?" joked Piper.

"I know! Fabulous, isn't it?"

"They won't even let us do selfies, Piper!" interrupted Suki.

Before social media doyen Piper could respond she was gowned and surrounded by two make-up artists and a hair stylist.

The ladies were ushered to the beautiful, contemporary lounge space with huge period windows, and massive flower arrangements. The continuity assistant snapped polaroids of the girls. Headshots, profiles and full length as the banter continued.

"Feel like Alexa Chung."

"I'm channeling Kate Moss!"

"I'm more Gwen Stefani..."

"In that case I'm Dande Stefano!" cackled Dande.

"Mrs Stefano? You two at least need to get engaged first? When's Eli gonna tie the knot?"

"I know - it's sooo boring! I can't wait to be Mrs Eli Stefano. Sounds good, dunnit? He won't do it though."

"My personal favourite is Nicole Richie."

Nancy changed the subject back to them, as it was a touchy subject for Dande.

"Here she comes!" announced Clara.

And with that Piper, the youngest and trendiest of them all sauntered into the room with the film crew gasping for breath. She was a knockout rocking Alberto Ferretti.

She made her brown hair with ash highlights work when it shouldn't. Her mate Craig was a colourist with a prestigious client list. The hair and makeup team created a loose up do, with a heavy fringe. The camera loved her profile, blessed with fine facial features and a natural pixie nose, natural unlike Nancy's bone straight one she'd had done. Her image greatly boosted her social media blogs. She was a slip of a thing. Possibly on the right side of a borderline eating disorder...or was it the gear? Every outfit, even the simplest jean ensemble was one she could catapult to couture status. By contrast, Suki was fashion forward in 'fugly' pieces, an Acne Studios addict. Whenever Piper donned oversized grey cashmere, skinny Paige jeans, old brogues no socks, she still exuded 'sexy as hell'.

"May as well go home now. You look drop dead gorge, Pi."

Nancy stood back.

"She's right, you do, Pi." curtsied Clara.

"What have they done to your hair? So nice!"

Suki curled her bottom lip in approval.

"Hope you don't go looking this good if I ever get married, missus. You're going to be my Maid of Honour one day, for fuck sake...hahaha..."

Dande looked on proudly at her little mate.

"Jeez guys! Was I that bad before?" Piper, torn by playing self-effacing nice and irked by the wedding reference.

"Great guys. Looking good!"

Edna finally showed her face alongside TV executives, directors, producers, assistant producers, set designers and more.

"Okay. Settle down everyone. I'm Dorrit, senior producer...we met in the office before? Listen carefully. What we're going to do today is take you to a product launch for sunglasses. They're going to be sold at all the coolest resorts in the world from Ibiza, Miami, to the Carribean, California and Aspen, etc..." This is the first reveal to suppliers and we would like to shoot you there. All you have to do is relax and enjoy yourselves...like you would at any event."

The ladies were quietly squealing at this point. Dorrit continued.

"The event will take place at the ME Hotel packed with loads of famous faces. The brand owner will not be named at this stage, but this is going to be a champagne-fuelled, high-end affair you will all enjoy. And please! Pace yourselves...haha...we won't miss a thing on camera. Now, remember, this is still a one-off, a pilot, so make sure you keep the energy going, as I'm sure you will. Good luck! I'll hand you over to Charlotte."

"Thank you Dorrit...hi guys, I'll be directing today. What I do is guide you to the right spots to stand in. I will cue you if I need you to talk about anything specific. Don't worry, I'll be there all the way. We can stop at any time if you feel uncomfortable. You'll soon pick up how it all works. Good luck from me too. My assistant Polly is on hand if you have any questions."

The TV people shook hands with each of the ladies and marched off, sweeping away with concerned expressions that threw anyone looking on.

As the chatter re-ignited Emilee sprang into action. "Guys, who still has their phones on them? I need to take those, thank you. Please put them on silent first."

"Can't we just leave them to the side? I need to check on the child minder."

"Yes, me too. My mum's not well."

The excuses came in, but they promptly gave in when Dande tried to explain 'showbiz' protocol.

"Sorry guys. You'll get them back. They'll be perfectly safe. Cheers."

Piper was the most reluctant, but was relieved she had already got her fix having spoken to her forbidden lover, Eli just before.

Suddenly it was all becoming very real, looking at each other, glowing, glamorously. The lights flooded the area they were positioned in with maximum daylight. The atmosphere pierced by that collective sense of knowing. Yes. The Housewives of House - they owned this shit. Too glam to give a damn!

"What are we meant to talk about?" dared Nancy... "Who's gonna go first?"

"I think we're meant to talk about the sunglasses event," said Dande taking the lead. "Can't wait for the launch party!"

"Me too. Wonder who'll be there?"

"We will be! We know how to get the party started girls, don't we?"

"Yes, Piper... partying is our lifeblood, after all!" said Dande. "We're not with superstar DJs for nothing!" she added cheesily.

"Oh no, we can't say that?"

Piper the most media savvy of the group sensed the cringy comment wouldn't go down well.

At that point a hand waving Polly ran over.

"Guys, listen, relax. It's all good. Just behave naturally. Why don't you, Dande and Piper, come with me. You can enter the group and kind of introduce each other. I know you all know one another, but we have to cheat it for now. Kind of say where and how you all met. Then after that you can talk about the event tonight. The brand is called Speculove."

Piper leaned in and whispered: "That sounds familiar, hmmm?"

The make-up team pounced and dabbed their faces. Suki, Nancy and Clara were prodded and shoved into their starting positions and warned not to stare at the cameras: whatever happened, they were going to keep the conversation flowing.

"Don't know about you, but I'm getting nervous now." Clara was full of foreboding.

"Me too. I feel stupid." Nancy was feeling the pressure as well.

"I know what you mean. Our stupidity should stay in-house. Now everyone is gonna know what we're really like!" Suki's comments weren't helping.

"Shssh, I think they can hear us. We've got mics on..."

"Well spotted, Nance, imagine we...anyhoo. Keeping schtum for now."

"Okay guys. When you're ready. We're gonna roll. Relax and just be your beautiful selves. Piper and Dande will walk in..." Polly looked to the props guy and yelled!

"Top ups for the girls please. More champers!"

Bass, How Low Can You Go

Can you get the package redirected to me please? I'm in Chertsey, Surrey. I have the tracking number…I'll pay the extra. Just need it done!"

Eli was at pains to get this delivery, part of a nice little deal he had going with the suppliers. He was about to take off to Ibiza for the start of the season, and was in the usual full-on rush to get organised. He was annoyed to be taking on domestic duties while Dande was away playing 'telly' the same day he needed her.

The recording studio was a bit out of the way from his west London base. But just far enough for Eli to escape the drudgery of home life, which he could only handle in small doses. He paid the huge mortgage, as far as he was concerned that was enough. Dande could crack on with the rest of the responsibilities. She made him a lovely home with great aplomb.

One of five brothers, the other Stefano boys had married and settled down. Eli was the youngest and keen to avoid this route. His relationship status thus far was 'car crash'. He had dated an ex-hooker (unbeknown to him at the time), after that, a lap dancer with another dubious past. She was a beauty and as usual he was all about looks. Character didn't come into play for him.

His son Bertram's mother was a crack addict, the

one least expected to let him down. The one-time IT girl, Amy Dunn, daughter of an actress mother. She had inherited notably high cheekbones from her and was elegant in her countenance. As she suffered with mental health linked to an erratic past, she battled with addictions and was failing disastrously. Losing custody of her son did not faze her. She had only one love in her life. Class As.

Eli had carried Amy's big addiction a secret for a long time and felt guilty for failing to save her. He had to leave her because circumstances forced him to. He would never have given up on her. Like all the others he cared for deeply, he was drawn to vulnerable women. Their helplessness appealed to his macho sense of 'manhood'. Being needed. After the relationship had ended, he made the mistake of sleeping with her. A mercy fuck, after he started dating Dande. His beloved Bertie was the result.

When his DJ career took off, he attracted more than his fair share of fans. His ego lapped this up. He saw this as the 'necessary evil' of the game he had to play to keep his name relevant, or so he reckoned. Like a rockstar, he had to have a fawning female fan base. DJ Elijah Stefano fans were not just for looking at.

He had been working with his producer mate, Jake Jockey, in the studio for years. They had been lucky from the off, and had a cult hit with their first release Booster Plus. It wasn't until after they had toured the track that they developed their craft. Striving to repeat the runaway success of that first hit, they had learned so much more and so the music became contrived as they tried too hard to replicate what they had done before. They were more like a married couple. Jake was low key and reliable. What Eli said went, except for the music. This was a shared passion on a more equal footing. Dande got used to having single man Jake around. He was made godfather to both of their kids.

"Listen, listen...wow!" enthused Jake. "When that bass drops man, gets me every time. I think we've cracked it again, fella."

"Mate, I'm still trying to get my delivery sorted."

Eli's feet wedged open the heavy studio doors. The phone signal was poor there. He hung up and jumped straight back into the leather swivel chair and grabbed a handful of Pringles. He rocked back and forth erratically as he swallowed mouthfuls of canned beer.

"Yes. Yes. Better. This is better, J man! What did you do there?"

"I took out the synths and brought this bit up. That's the Ravanne drum. Listen..."

Jake showed off his production wizardry. This was the arena where he could always impress his buddy. But on the decks Eli came into his own. He had charisma that shy Jake could only dream about. That brash confidence was a far cry from his studious personality.

"Ah mate! That's serious!"

Eli sprang from his seat and started a two-step fist pump action on the beat of the music.

"Lively, huh?"

"Mix this down now. It's ready. Whoop."

"I'll have this done next couple hours, you hanging about?"

"For a bit. I have to head back to pick up this parcel. Bastards wouldn't redirect, but they're dropping it off at a later time instead. Tell you what... they'd better."

"Yeah...fuckers!"

"Don't think Dande and the rest are due back 'til late. That filming stuff can run on and on…"

"How you feeling about all that? You think it's good for us? I mean it sounds a bit naff?"

"I know what you mean. But you can't beat TV publicity. If the music is hot, nothing can stop it, man. Dande is full of it, though. She wants it so badly. Never seen her like this. It's all she talks about, that, and…er…getting hitched."

"Ah, that's Dande's alright. If she's happy…but what's with Piper, then? You're getting out of your depth there, fella."

"I keep trying to end it with her. I don't know how we keep…I dunno. She's trouble. I actually think I sort of love them both!"

"Elijah, Elijah Stefano, no no no no! This will not end well. I don't have your player instincts, but you can't shag your girl's best mate and get away with it. How d'ya sleep? Think of Dande and the kids…and what about Charlie? I love all of ya."

Eli reaches his big arms across his pal's back. Then scrunched his neck as he placated him.

"Jake, baby. You worry wart. I've got this, okay? You ever known me not to come out smiling?"

"Err, yes. And quite a few times actually!"

"Alright, alright. Don't say it, please."

"Nah, I'm gonna! Amy! Yes, Amy?"

"Have you got my back J? That's low bro. Not cool."

"Sorry mate. I'm out of order. Just don't want to see you in that dark place again, yeah?"

The mixing desk volume then got whacked up at that bassline again, which nearly blew Eli's home-made speakers. Those beer stained bassbins were his pride and joy. The duo were back in their element.

The Pilot Continues

Nancy, Clara and Suki had found their form and were full flow in conversation to the point where they had forgotten they were on camera. Just at that biting point in walked Dande and Piper.

"Hey, hey," they all exclaimed collectively, air kissing and holding shoulders.

Dande was straight in as directed.

"Nice to see you all again. You all know me, Dande and you've all met Piper, right?"

The fake theatrics got turned up to ten.

"Yes, I'm Clara and I met Nancy and Suki at a gig your hubby Charlie Fenchurch was playing at in Ibiza a zillion years ago." she said pointing at Piper. "But we met briefly before, though, didn't we Dande?"

Clara pointed to her friends.

We've all known each other for a good while now. It's nice," added Suki.

"Yes, it's great we get to hang out, especially at Dande's when the boys are away!" replied Piper.

"Aw, I love having you guys come over, but it's so nice to be out and about. What about this launch then?"

"The Speculove launch...hope there're some goodie bags."

"There's bound to be. Sounds ace!"

"I wonder who'll be there?!"

"As long as the champagne is flowing, who cares?

I'm in the mood for a good party"

"It's still a product launch. I wonder who's behind it?"

"Right!" came a massive screech. "We'll cut it there!"

The startled women paused for a moment and then went straight back into chatter mode, not realising the cameras were still rolling.

Piper was straight in. "I recognise that name. I think it's Sugar St Jean's brand, you know?"

"No way...you're joking, aren't you?"

"I'm definitely not going if it's her thing."

"Are you sure, Piper?"

"No, I'm not sure. I have a hunch. There's been a buzz over social media about some new shades being launched by her. Could so easily be this one."

"Not surprising, really, considering she's a shady fuck!"

They howled at her comment.

"So what we gonna do if it IS her?"

"I'm walking straight out. I don't care. I can't stand the bitch!"

"Guys, guys calm down. We're working ourselves up over nothing. We don't know if it's her yet."

"Dande, we hate her as much as you do. Are you able to be in the same room as her?"

"Yes. She will hate us being there! Flip reverse it on her."

"If the products are cheap crap I'm going to say so!"

"Hmmm. I'm so wound up now."

"Here, fill up your glasses, it's going to be a long evening. Really hope it's not her!"

Watching with glee, on the monitors out of sight were the executive producer, Gillian Morris-Quaid,

TV-Edna and someone from continuity.

Out marched Polly again, screeching "Stop there!"

"Okay ladies. Well done," responded Edna patronisingly.

"That's your first bit of filming done," she added before they could get a word in. "How does it feel?"

The buzz of crew packing up and shuffling about took hold and the ladies were ushered up to the dressing room where more rails had been brought in with even more fancy clobber. Reena was still loitering about building up her part.

Brocades, velvets and silk, muted colours from light sage, off white and vintage rose hung like a treasure trove amid the wrapping tissues and artsy labels.

Once again the girls were excited, rifling through the best haute couture boutique ever. They discretely glanced over for Reena's approval as they held up items from satin hangers. Her expression had the air of a Roman emperor with a pompous thumbs up or down. Georgio and Lucy shrugged at Sofia as they tried to keep to their brief.

Ever-ready Emilee waltzed in, amidst the hullaballoo, with the confiscated mobile phones.

"Okay ladies...here are your phones. I won't collect them again until we get to the next venue."

"Look at that? 18 missed calls!" exclaimed Dande.

"I've got 21 missed calls and about a million texts!" followed Clara.

"Same here!"

"It's only gonna get worse!"

Meantime, Piper was staring at her phone scrolling through her own messages. Mostly from her husband...and her mum. Nothing from Eli.

"Hazard of the job," mumbled Piper.

"I told everyone I was unavailable all day today, so I'm good," bragged Suki.

"I'm just gonna make a quick call everyone," announced Nancy.

"Me too."

"I'll come with..."

Emilee had lost 'the talent'...and at the exact wrong moment. Polly had followed her and was seething at her stupidity.

"Guys, guys don't disappear! Choose your outfits..." Polly paused before adding "...first."

The women had all vanished to seek their own quiet corner of the house.

"Great!" continued Polly, snapping at Emilee.

"Sorry. I'll go and round them up."

"Think, next time. They could have had their phones after the break."

"I just thought..."

"It's done now! Tch!"

The stylists Georgio and Lucy sarcastically bowed their heads and looked away. It was awkward.

Pilot Evening

"Okay, Suki, you're going to walk up to the venue, then pause just as you see Nancy and Clara coming towards you. Chat briefly...then we'll shoot you all walking in together. Don't over think it. Just a simple 'hi, you look nice' and excitement about the launch. Once we're inside we'll come back to you."

Polly looked over at Nancy and Clara.

"Hope you caught that guys. Wave to Suki at the door, okay?"

Staying with Acne Studios wearing their cross-body bag and shoes, Suki wiggled her legs in anticipation.

She had picked out a Viktor & Rolf frill jacket and felt like a hundred million Hong Kong dollars! Glossed with product, her recently chopped asymmetric fringe with a flash of red and matching lips was in keeping with her current style sensibilities.

The lights lit up the warm evening sky and the showbiz haze added to the atmosphere. Paparazzi took their positions. Just another night's work for them.

Once inside, Dande and Piper propped up at the bar next to a high table filled with products and booze. The young nubile cocktail waiters were in shot in their white and green palm print, open Hawaiian shirts, flashing their cut torsos.

Trying not to tilt pressure from one foot to the other, Dande and Piper stood upright in a way only seriously high heels can inspire. Dande went for Armani flared straight trousers and cotton flared Armani top. Marni footwear and Celine bag completed the chic look. Piper wore black chiffon by Philosophy, a black leather pencil skirt by Miu Miu and red stilettos by Nicholas Kirkwood.

The venue was excruciatingly noisy with music, loud voices talking over each other and the clanging of glasses and bottles. The girls had been fitted with mic packs to pick up their conversations.

They had been standing, waiting so long that Dande and Piper completely forgot they were filming. It was just another 'do' for them. Charlie Fenchurch and Elijah Stephano were not short of DJ spots at event gigs themselves, reluctantly for the money. Their partners enjoyed them, though. Otherwise, they would avoid those jobs. They were too cool for them. However, the big pay cheques and the less effort needed at these events, meant sneering at them was foolhardy.

"Piper. I can see her from here. Ten to two."

"She here? So it IS her thing then!"

Piper tried to spy innocuously.

"Sugar St-flaming-Jean. Whatta bitch! I can't talk to her. She's evil!"

"From what you told me, I won't talk to her either. I've got your back, don't worry. If she comes over here, I'll rescue you!"

"Thanks, Pi. Stop me from swinging for her. Please!"

Purse lipped, Dande swallowed more champagne from the coupe glass.

"Oh, here come the girls!"

Piper nodded towards the back of a jam-packed room.

"Hiya! Mwaw."

"Beautiful. You look gorgeous."

"Mwaw. Gorge, gorge, gorgeous."

"Heyyy. This is nice."

Dande beckoned the strategically placed silver service waitress in and handed everyone a glass.

"So, have we missed anything?" pressed Suki.

"No, not yet. But a lot of the Ibiza massive is here," added Piper.

"Bloody hell. Really good turnout. Especially with the season about to start."

"Who's playing?"

"Think it's Jesmond Harrison, can't quite make out."

"Hmmm," groaned Dande. "It must be him. Sugar St Jean is hosting. It's her launch!"

"Oh no, Dand." Nancy covered her mouth, her bold Balenciaga gold cuff glinted. "Of course. I always forget you went out with him. I know you hate Sugar, but I forget why sometimes. Even though she is a bitch regardless."

"She stole him right from under me. All those lies she said about me being a caner, just to take him off me. I can't fucking stand her."

"Oh, oh...here she comes..." whispered Clara, in a plunged back Gucci jumpsuit.

"Hi, gorgeous ladies. Lovely to see you all looking so glamorous. Hope you're enjoying yourselves."

She sounded like the Wicked Witch Of The West.

The girls, not a sound between them, simply nodded. Grimaced smiles and raised eyebrows the only acknowledgement they could muster.

"Oh, make sure you take a goodie bag before you leave. Hope to see you on the White Isle again, soon. Hahahaha..."

Sugar St Jean patted Clara on her naked back as she left.

"Grrrrr! One of these days. I swear!" fumed Dande.

"Well done, well done, hun. You didn't rise to the bait!"

"I don't feel any better for it, though."

"Just think you wouldn't have met Eli. Look how happy you two are!"

"Still doesn't make me feel any better. I was in love with Jes, you know. She told him I was an alcoholic mess and a gold digger! He believed her."

"It's upsetting Dande. I understand why it's hard to forget."

"She's swanning around with MY ex like she fucking owns the place. I bet he's behind the business or at least one of his cronies is. Arrrrgh!"

"No one's got anything nice to say about her. You're not alone," A Chloe dress-wearing Nancy assured, tapping her Phillip Lim ankle booted feet.

"I know. Thanks guys. Love you," said Dande, hugging them all individually.

The music stopped, the mic feedback tolled and Sugar St Jean in her white on white sequinned jumpsuit stood at the allocated space next to her product stand.

Her scrawny arms outstretched pointing to her sunglasses range.

"Good evening everyone! How the hell are you all doing? I'm so glad you could all be here for my first ever product launch. Hah! I'm so nervous...for those of you that know me, you know that I am never without a pair of my trusty shades. And I'm always asked about my style when I'm on the road with Jessy! Mwaw. Love you darling."

Dande mimed the barfing gesture.

"Your support throughout this process has been humbling," continued Sugar St Jean. "Love you maan! So, it just seemed the right time to create my own range. Hope you're all going to love them! As a way of saying thank you for coming tonight, there are goodie bags for you all at the back. Ladies and Gentlemen, I give you Speculove!"

The crowd whooped and clapped. The Housewives of House made tiny two finger claps in solidarity of Dande.

"Ok! That was great!"

Once again the girls jumped when Charlotte and Polly showed up.

"We've got most of what we need girls. If you want to hang out a while longer feel free to do so."

"We will send for the clothes in the week. Please take care of them. You can't keep them…sorry!"

Stylist Sofia was on hand, ready to confiscate the Fendi, Celine, Acne, Balenciaga and YSL bags and accessories.

"Come with me guys," she insisted, but before she could do it they were led to a spot in the foyer for both continuity and publicity shots. A makeup lady appeared from nowhere.

The Housewives of House lined up and people started pointing and wondering who they were. Some did not care, they wanted selfies all the same.

Dande was in her element, basking in the glorious attention.

Soon there were paparazzi taking photos for daily online newspapers.

"Just imagine…," mused Dande. "It could be like this all the time, if we got a series! I mean we could literally become famous after this. It's what I've been dreaming about forever, Clara."

"Tonight has been great, but it still scares me. It

would be hard to get used to all this, all of the time...
once in a while maybe."

"I'm definitely getting my teeth done," added
Dande, confidently. "If this pilot gets commissioned,
that is."

"Like Edna's...hahaha!"

"I wouldn't mind if it meant we could keep the
clothes and handbags!"

"Well that is the upside."

"Let's shut up and take the photos, shall we?"

"Everyone say 'hardcore!'" demanded Clara.

"No, say 'Housewives of House'."

Just as the girls were basking in the spotlight as a
collective for the first time, dreaming about the
endless opportunities ahead, in swept Sugar St Jean
like a gust of wind.

Beckoning her own personal photographer, she
shoved herself smack in between them, stooping
down in an icy courtesy with her spindly white
sequined, catsuit-legged self.

"Ladeeez. Just the one picture," said Sugar, holding up a goodie bag with her 'Speculove' branding
emblazoned over it.

"Just a couple more please!" ordered one scruffy
old photographer.

"Okay. Let's make it count," croaked Sugar.

Dande scowled. No way was she about to comply
further. They had been wrapped after all. In her
annoyance she turned about face and excused herself, to the ladies toilets unable to contain her anger
at the humiliation she was internalising.

All the others followed. Sugar St Jean pretended
not to notice, secretly smug she had successfully
instigated Dande's tantrum.

Charlotte, having caught the tail end of this,

radioed through to the single cameraman, Paul, who was nearest to the washroom and directed him to shoot whatever followed. Immediately the lighting and camera op assumed the position at the toilet doors, waiting for the talent to feed their lens.

Hobbling at maximum speed, shoving past VIPs and personalities, Dande got madder and madder. The red mist fell, promising an explosion.

"Leave me!" said Dande, pushing Piper's hand away.

"Don't do this, D. Please. Wait."

"She's fucking with me. She's taking the piss!"

Suki hurried round. "Babe, babe..."

But it was no use. There was no consoling her. She had already downed a few sambuca shots at the bar on top of champagne.

"If I'd've known this was her thing! Fuckkk! I need a line!"

"That's not the answer, hun. You can't do that here."

The camera rolled.

Piper gently brushed Dande's arm, again trying to get through to her.

"Seriously. Have you got a line or not? Whose side are you on anyway?"

Dande's infamous paranoia began to set in.

"Oh, don't start, babe. It's all been going so nicely," Piper assured her.

"Yeah, you must've known. You and your social media shit. It must've been out there. It's all a set up, isn't it?"

Clara and Nancy clawed their way in to save the degenerating situation fast.

"Oh, ho, ho, no you don't, Dande," screamed Nancy. "Don't get angry with me. This is yours and

Sugar's problem. Don't drag us into this!"

"Get that out of my face!" raged Dande, her fist flailing at the camera op.

Assisted by Clara, Nancy tried to Heimlich hold Dande, already unsteadily tottering in her shoes.

Piper snarled at Dande in disbelief at what was happening.

"You're in on it, Piper. You've been sneaking about on that phone and suddenly hanging up. I've seen you. Something is going on and you're in on it. Fuck you!"

"What are you on about?" said Piper, following the huddle of girls out of the ladies, just as Sugar St Jean was entering.

"What's all this? Dande pissed again?" laughed Sugar St Jean.

Dande lunged at Sugar's platinum extensions and yanked at them. The black-suited security took over and lifted her safely away, holding her arms down. She immediately retreated, insisting she could walk without the manhandling.

Sugar looked back at her with disgust, ostentatiously fanning herself with her black Coutts credit card and air snorted her right nostril with her thumb as she continued to the ladies to rack up her own 'line'.

Dande sat in a nearby empty function suite, quietly cooling down and sobbing.

"Where's my phone? Call Eli, I want Eli," she sobbed. Her beautifully coiffed hair belied her anguish. She knew she had overreacted. She knew it was childish. It had been a long while since she had an outburst like this one. But she couldn't live this one down because it had all been captured on camera. The shame of it just twisted her into knots of frustration. Would Piper forgive her and had she ruined their chances with the show? How could she let Sugar St Jean get the better of her yet again?

The 'Housewives' circled around her. With words that they hoped would comfort.

"We love you, Dande. We don't like seeing you like this, hun."

"You are so much better than her and she knows it."

"She was determined to provoke you, I reckon. I'd have reacted the same."

Barely able to be in the same room, much less look at her, Piper leaned up against the wall tapping her fingers against her thigh. Making eye contact with the others, furiously nodding her head incredulously.

"It's getting late. We'll leave this for now and get you all home," said Charlotte sternly. "We've booked you all a cab each. We suggest you leave whatever this is here and let's talk about it in the next meeting. Anyway ladies, these things happen. Emilee will hand you back the phones. Thank you for today."

Charlotte left the room, but turned at the doorway. "On no account do any of you re-enter the event! Hope this is understood!"

The ladies all looked down at their designer clad feet, like unruly sheepish sixth formers.

"Hand back the phones, Emilee. Quick as you can," ordered Polly.

Sofia walked round the girls solemnly collecting the clutch purses for a basket weave bag full of handbag dust bags. She needed to get these highly sought-after couture items back in one piece. She inspected each item for damage as they handed them over.

Dande snatched her iPhone from the intern's tray and speed-dialled Eli.

"Babe, babe..." she sniffled as she rose from her chair and picked up her tatty Mulberry 'Bayswater' bag from the pile of stuff on the table.

"What's up babe? What's happened?"

"Eli...Eli..."

She broke down, sorting her belongings searching for her leather All Saints jacket.

Feeling ashamed, with Eli still on the phone, she waved half a goodbye to the room, mouthing a wimpish 'thank you' before leaving.

"Babe! Talk to me! What the hell happened? Why're you crying?"

"It was horrible! That fucking bitch turned up! I hate her!"

Eli was back at home and perched on the bed. She could only be referring to one person.

"Amy? What was she doing there?"

"Why is everything about fucking Amy Dunn! I don't give a fuck about Amy! Fuck sake!"

"Calm down. Hate hearing you like this. Are you on your way home?"

Eli was concerned about the pilot's turn of events.

"I'm just getting in a cab now."

"What's wrong? Tell me, Dandelion!"

"Sugar. Sugar St Jean. It was her thing," revealed Dande.

"Whaaaat? Why didn't they tell you?"

"I know. They kept it from me and I had a really bad row with Piper as well..."

"Listen, hush, shssh, shssh... never mind, babe. Try not to talk about anything in the cab...you're nearly famous now, darling. You gotta watch what you say in public..."

Eli took a chance to appease her with that, but despite the sour outcome he could barely hear.

"Okay...why do I...?"

"Shssh, tell me when you get in. We'll have a night cap and go over it. Just try and chill out in the taxi."

"Do you have to fly out in the morning? Can't you move it? Love you, you know that?"

"Hey, you know the answer to that. Love you too..."

The Five-Go-Hard WhatsApp was ablaze with gossip about the shoot and the subsequent fall out. The day they had been building up to. A day that had began early that morning but already felt like 48 hours...Their happy ambition now had a crack in it. Could they sustain the damage, they wondered?

It was divisive to the group when Dande accused Piper of setting them up. Edna Wright was the more likely suspect, but Piper was guilty of bringing her in. They argued between themselves, and thus most empathised with Dande's suspicions, as misguided as they seemed. Piper, meanwhile, was texting Eli in the middle of the WhatsApp frenzy.

"D went batshit crazy tonight! Why are you still with her? Speak tomorrow. Love you."

*****

"Did you get all that, Paul?" asked Charlotte.

"Yup! Every last frame of it!" bragged the Portable Single Cameraman (PSC).

"It's good...very good. And amazing for a pilot!"

"Great, I almost thought we were going to have to plot another 'bump in'...anyhoo, thanks for that. Can't wait to see the rushes!"

Charlotte was very pleased with herself. Her instinct for a sensationalist sting was 'awe' winning! Still on radio, she called on Polly, Edna and the rest of the team to join her at Grouchos for "a late tipple" on her. Everyone had to attend. That's the way it is. Work hard. Play hard. She had a family in Hertford-shire to head back to. But that's the way she ran her shows. On adrenalin. Relentlessly.

The Pilot Hangover

Snuggled in bed, with a bottle of Sambuca to her side on a Moroccan mother of pearl inlaid side table, Dande was under Eli's huge arms. She had finished explaining her version of the event.

"Babe, don't go in hard on Piper. She's your mate. That's all I'll say. She couldn't have set you up. Think it over. There're too many variables. It's those TV people, if you ask me. They do their homework. If they were looking for your nemesis it wouldn't take much, would it? Everyone on the scene knows you and Sugar got beef..." Eli's opinions were not being well received as Dande pulled away a bit.

She looked up sternly at him.

"What? What? Don't look at me like that? You know everyone knows about you and Jesmond. He's a face. Are you pissed 'cos you ended up with me? Because that's what it sounds like to me. Thought it was behind us. Bloody years ago!"

"What, you think I'm jealous of that cow? She accused me of being a gold digger and a lush! He believed her, though. It's unforgivable."

"I get it, hun. I don't wanna argue with you. It's this victim stance, hun. Nobody is out to get you. I'm here. I love you. The kids love you too. It's all good. Focus on that."

"If we were a proper family, married for instance, I suppose I would focus on that."

"I know I rushed in on you when Jesmond left you, I didn't have that much to offer you then. Him a superstar DJ with his flash model/actress girlfriends, flash car and flash gifts. But it's all superficial, darl...doesn't mean anything. I thought you were the most beautiful thing I'd ever seen. I had to have you. Why do you wanna worry about that scraggy, tore up witch following him about?"

"Tore up! Hahaha...She was in white on white sequins tonight. She looked like a cotton bud dipped in glitter! Hehehe..."

Once again Eli had turned things around and made Dande laugh at the end of it.

"You know Jesmond is screwing Georgette Jonsson on the sly? Don't say anything, but she is preggers too... hahaha..." add Eli, ignoring any kind of boy code...or his own indiscretions.

"Noooo! Georgette? She's just beautiful. Can't be more than 23? He's sick!"

"Her mother is fuming. It will be in the papers soon."

"Her mother is doing a stint in that play I told you about at The Young Vic. Could be publicity for that. But she'll be pissed. What's wrong with him? He's twice her age!"

"Told you, D. You shouldn't hold onto stuff. The world keeps moving on."

She thumped him playfully. "Why didn't you tell me before? I'd love to have looked that cow in the eye with this juice!"

"Ouch! Don't say anything. I've broken the DJ Code telling you, as it is. Keep this under your hat. I mean it."

They kissed, he switched the side lamp off.

"Eli...babe?" whispered Dande. "Was that a pro-posal?"

"Will you shut up and go to sleep? I've got a plane to catch in a few hours..."

"Yes. I will marry you!"
"Not this again...go to sleep. Nutter!"
Eli gave her a loving squeeze.

Piper's Plight

Piper was licking her wounds after Dande's attack and looked to Charlie for reassurance. But he was playing out that night. She could not leave a message as he never had his voicemail activated. He had two phones. But he could not be reached. The WhatsApp convo with the girls did not offer her enough appeasement. The pain was exacerbated by not being able to reach out to Eli either. Piper sobbed the rest of the journey home in the car, with a sickening pining in her stomach. The only place she wanted to be was in Eli's arms. She hugged herself to hold in the angst of it, as the driver seemed to ram into every speed bump taking the 'back doubles' route to her home.

She opened the gigantic front door of her Westbourne Grove three-storey townhouse and ran upstairs to relieve the babysitter and order her a cab. As soon as she had left, Piper crept into her children's rooms, Luke and Poppy, and gently kissed them goodnight while they slept.

Across the corridor she entered her locked dressing room, opened the safe and pulled out a flea-bitten velvet necklace box. She sniffed a little heap of white powder using the metal straw inside. She carefully placed everything back. Locked the safe and took herself to her super king sized bed. Still fully clothed, she gazed up at her ceiling, the tree shadows cast by the streetlights dancing over the plantation shutters.

Her beautiful babies sound asleep in their rooms, a walk-in closet full of vintage and stylish contemporary clothes, shoes and bags aplenty; an Aga fitted open plan kitchen, the Porsche Cayenne, a part time nanny, a figure people would eat their right arm for, a devoted husband of some 11 years. She pondered over her many blessings. Why wasn't it enough?

Her bleary eyes just longed for the one thing she did not have. Eli. The warmth and intimacy that Eli gave her in and out of the bedroom. If anyone should find out about their affair, it was going to be a disastrous tower moment...according to the tarot anyway. She was ready for that showdown.

She convinced herself that her kids would adjust to Eli as a step-father easily. He was an affectionate guy. Nurturing. However long it took, once everyone accepted that she and Eli were a couple, it would be worth it for the eventual happy outcome. Loads of people do it. She was better for him than that AA reject Dande and his previous, crack-HAD-IT girl, Amy Dunn.

Dande was too selfish and domineering for him. The frustration erupted within Piper again. How could she look into Charlie's eyes and admit to this betrayal? Eli could take the flack for her and get her off the hook. She plotted this and multiple scenarios in her mind, amounting to many lost hours every day since they first made love. A 'bit of fun' became a 'thing'.

They never tell you this at the Affair Academy.

That first time, when friendly banter and laughter sparks a bolt flash of chemistry between two and ascends into breathless passion.

Piper's huge saucer eyes had met Eli's crafty gaze.

It was only a matter of when. They both knew it.

That first time. Piper dared to look behind her as he unflinchingly stared right back.

That first time. The rush of adrenaline shot through her heart when he brushed his hand across her lower back.

That first time. The nerve endings bristled when the opportunity presented itself. They had lost their partners in Ibiza. Easily done after DC10... both their phones dead. The cab took them to the harbour in Santa Eulària. The keys to a boat. A friend's boat who was away in Dénia for a few days.

That first time. She was intoxicated by more than the drugs and cocktails. She never felt like this before.

That first time. He lay on top of her. His hands, such big hands like silk feathers tracing her torso in a tenderness unexpected of the man she knew.

That first time. His heaving solid six pack, heavily breathing.

That first time. Pinned down inside, gripped by girth, gliding with each ebb and flow of the sea waves outside.

That first time. Mesmerised by this act of love. She saw how he took his time with her. He wanted her to enjoy him. He needed to see it.

That first time. He lowered himself, arms out-stretched towards her arms, tasting her nipples. She almost succumbed to its sublime pleasure.

That first time. Under the moonlit sky on the bed, his tongue danced from her navel and brushed her pubic runway. How he widened and whirled his pink wonder over her exposed flower, seeking the folding, flesh of petals, arranging her by her groans.

That first time. On the verge of a momentous moan, he had waited for.

That first time. He knew that now she was ready for the growth he had become.

That first time. She did not know she was ready to receive him teetering on the aching to come. He tilted himself, gathered purchase to see himself all in. He held it there. The top of the rollercoaster, rocking side to side before the glorious withdrawal. Each laboured insertion was better than the last, the last being perfect.

That first time. She was able to acknowledge an intimate connection with a man that seemed to discover her from the inside for the very first time.

That first time.

At dawn they got into the only cab in sight and playfully tickled each other on the way back to the apartments they were all staying in that season. It does not matter what lame excuses each gave their partners. It's the White Isle. Rearrange the letters and it becomes the White Lies where the unexpected is expected.

Piper cried herself into her mass of luxury pillows. At a loss as to why she was known by her blog name 'Piper Blair Doesn't Care'. She did care…very much. Her social media fame went before her. Resented by DJ WAGs and DJ WAGs: Housewives of Houses worldwide and what for? She never quite understood. DJ Charlie Fenchurch, a high achiever and a great provider, did everything but make her feel loved. Emotionally detached, she gave up trying to connect with him. He loved her like an inanimate object. He was materialistic and enjoyed nice things. From cars, to state-of-the-art audio tech equipment dotted about the home and the basement recording studio.

Charlie would shower her with jewelery and handbags when she started complaining. Mostly about his detachment from her and the family. He never got it. As long as he ensured they had more than enough, what other kind of love was there for him to show? The best holidays in the finest resorts, from Seychelles to Dubai or St Barts and Miami. On these trips away he doted on his kids and saw this as 'the quality time'. Naturally while on holiday he would try and secure a gig over one of the nights, but "just the one".

Their premium residence in Westbourne Grove housed all his awards in pride of place over the studio's soundproofed walls. A gorgeous wife and beautiful son and daughter, in a luxurious home with several V8 engine motors, were all Charlie's boxes ticked. He was at the top of his game. What more could he be expected to give?

Piper could not go on taking. How could she... once she had experienced the passion with sure-footed Eli? The connection with him was an all-en-compassing energy that took on more importance to her than her stable family life. Her children were demanding. She often admitted they were spoiled brats, though, but nowhere as bad as Eli's Bertie.

Unable to sustain being the horrible parent who said "no" all the time, Charlie always undermined her and succumbed to the children's endless material requests whenever he came back from a tour or gig.

Little Luke and Poppy ruled the roost.

They knew the exact time to ask their Dad for the next big 'must have'. He felt love by indulging them. The rows Piper and Charlie had never lasted long because Charlie would shut down and roll out his stock quote: "I'm not discussing this now, with you." Then he would coldly shoot off. Point blank refuse to engage with her by either retreating to the studio or leaving the house.

Piper was left rattling around in her W11 ivory tower...and the rattle was getting louder.

They would sulk and snarl at each other, no words, until their parental responsibilities forced them back together, united at a school event or via sleepover plans or for a family occasion.

The glowing picture-perfect advert of West London living was increasingly becoming a façade. The buildup of resentment was taking its toll on the Fenchurchs.

*****

After Dande waved Eli and his precious new vinyl flight cases off for his Ibizan residency, she tried to round up the girls for the obligatory catch-up and pick up the proverbial pieces of the night before. Rather than text, she rang round each of the group, inviting them to hers for a sushi lunch she would order in. This bribe rarely failed. All responded favourably except Piper who didn't pick up.

Suki had already done the rounds that morning dropping off the group's kids to various schools, as she always did after heavy nights and in emergencies. Dande primed her to bring Piper on her way back through.

"Pi, it's me Suki. I'm outside, let me in."

"Sorry yes, hun...the kids get to school okay?"

"I said I'd come back through, open the door, hun."

Piper was fully dressed. She tore herself away from a hot laptop, writing another piece for her blog page. Having to constantly share her daily shenanigans was becoming a chore. She had looked forward to journaling last night's launch with the camera crew, but Dande's storming off had created a stench she couldn't shift. There was no chance of the piece coming out objectively. Her emotions and her relationship with Eli was clouding everything she did. She didn't know why she was suddenly struggling to keep the affair secret after all this time.

"Darling..."

"Alright, alright, Suks."

She peered out the large door.

"You not dressed?"

"What's up Suki? Thanks for dropping the kids off. Whatever it is, I'm not going."

With that Suki pushed through the door and stood in the hallway, tutting at her glam mate.

"You know very well why I'm here. I won't take no for an answer. Let's sort this out. Sooner the better. You and Dande never fall out. What's got into you both? Where's your jacket?"

"You don't understand," despaired Piper.

"Shsh! We're having shushi...hahaha...and it's on Dande! Get your keys...let's go!"

* * * * *

The late May sun shyly hid behind the clouds, but a few meagre rays had dramatic effect through the dome skylight of the riyadh-styled conservatory, which lent itself seamlessly to the French country kitchen with a contemporary twist. Dande had visited Agadir, Essaouira and Marrakech for inspiration countless times.

The reclaimed wooden table seated a dozen comfortably with a bench at one side. Bum-sized leather pillow pads scattered along for comfort. The rough-clefted, natural slate tiled floor enhanced the rustic charm of the space. The apron front copper sink by Herbeau was a conversation point. In fact, the whole house was a nod to Louis Herbeau and art nouveau design.

A set of six Stolix stools stood discretely tucked away under the essential must-have kitchen 'island', where the girls often sat amid an array of make-up jars, prosecco bottles and eco water bottles...Dande's new obsession. This was where they would have the sushi, perched on the stools keenly, leaning on their elbows. Nancy and Clara helped Dande brew some coffee over the stove, threw some spelt bread in the Aga and prepped some dips for the pre-lunch eats. The sushi delivery couldn't be ordered until noon and it would take at least 45 minutes to arrive.

"So, how've you left it with Piper?"

"I dunno. I'm so disgusted with myself. What was I thinking?"

"Well, Clara and I think it best you build fences, no I mean, mend bridges...is that right? That doesn't sound right?"

"Build bridges...yes, I know. That's why I'm doing this..."

"Well, we know you don't do the sushi spread for nothing!"

The trio glanced at each other with light chuckles, trying to read the appropriate mood in the camp.

"Ooh! Just got a text back from Suki. She's got Piper with her."

"Don't make that face, Dande, we have to smooth this out. Not taking sides. Remember we're doing TV."

"I know."

Dande was entering passive aggressive territory.

"Clara's right. Play nice. There's a lot riding on this. Whatever has got into you two?"

The fresh baked smell of the warmed spelt bread filled the kitchen, with fresh coffee overtones any bistro in Queen's Park would be proud of.

"Mmmm...let's tuck in. Don't do bread, but will make an exception."

"Nance, we're not listening! You always say that and then you gobble up those carbs quick smart!"

"Leave her alone. Try this butter I got from the farmers market...yum, so nice."

The friendly banter continued over the crudités and dips when they shrieked as something sounded like a ceiling crashing in. It was Bertram, with his massive rucksack and digital paraphernalia.

"Hey..." yelled Dande, as she ran to the staircase. "Are you bunking off again?!"

"I'm going out," grunted the teenager.

"Hi Bertie, come and say hello to Auntie Clara."

"Come say hello, Bert," followed Auntie Nance.

Their light tones failed to appease the stress in the atmosphere.

"Going where? If you're not off school, you'll stay put. Get back upstairs! As soon as your dad's back is turned you start. I'm not in the mood!"

"You can't stop me," yelled back Bertie

"Bertie!"

Dande was enraged knowing that Bertie predictably played up as soon as Eli flew out.

"Seeya..."

Bertie slammed the door shut behind him, pushing past Suki and Piper at the gate. They too were alarmed at the heavy energy he displayed. They could hear Dande shouting as she re-opened the door in response to the boy.

"Bertram, you get back here...now! Oh?"

"Hey Dande, boy trouble?" enquired Suki.

"Hi guys. Sorry about that. Bertie's acting up now Eli's gone. I swear I could...anyway. Come in, come in."

A purse-lipped Piper nodded and followed Suki in.

"Ooh something smells nice."

"It's the spelt bread, darling. Try some."

"Thanks, Nance."

Suki tore into the bun and wrestled it into her mouth.

"Mmmm...that's...mmmm."

Her mouthful hindered her speech.

The awkwardness was beginning to take shape as they reseated and shuffled about the food-ladled island.

"I'll put some music on." Dande made her escape to the corner for the remote, where the built-in sound resided, rolling her eyes to herself and chewing her bottom lip.

"Ah, that's better! Love this one."

Nancy got up, bouncing herself side to side to the groove.

"Coffee, guys?" enquired Clara, taking the lead.

"Help yourselves, you know where everything is. This is just a snackette 'til the sushi arrives."

"You know what we need? A little shot of something in this coffee."

"Clara!"

"What? Just saying..." added Clara. "I think a drop of Disaronno wouldn't go amiss!"

"Yeah. Why not? I'll get it. Your wish is my command, ladies!"

Dande was relieved she hadn't come up with the idea, even though she was gagging for a wee dram of something herself.

The snifter seemed to work a treat as they seemed to relax and chuckle more readily, although the underlying tension was ever present.

"When are the rest of the guys off again?" groaned Dande. "Eli left this morning."

"I can't wait! Think Flemming leaves Sunday. We've got his mother's big birthday lunch before…"

"Same, think Razr's going to that."

"Flemming ordered one of his Bonsai trees as a gift for her rockery."

"I'm not sure, think Baxta's got a few days before he heads out. Get the place to myself…fank-fuck!" mocked Nancy.

Suki finally braved the small talk with her opening gambit.

"So what did everyone think of last night? Yesterday, I mean!"

Nancy was seated. "I know my feet are still sore. We did a lot of standing up you know. They don't tell you that!"

"Loved those shoes, though," added Clara. "I loved every minute. Didn't feel like we were being filmed, did it?"

"Yeah, had a party feel to it, I thought," assured Suki nervously. "Showbiz suits me, ha!"

"What about you Dande?" ventured Nancy. "You looked amazing!"

"Thanks, hun. It was all going so well. Still wish I knew that Sugar St Jean was featuring in events. That spoiled it for me."

"Yeah, that was pants! But who cares about that bitch anyway. It's our show, don't forget."

Clara was quick to back up her mate.

"Yes, I agree. The bigger picture. Literally, haha,"

conceded Dande, adding... "Eli was so nice when I got back. He made me see sense."

At that she turned to Piper, who was studying her own phone.

"Piper, I'm sorry about last night. Can't believe I got so worked up..."

"Well, you did say some hurtful things. I don't know where it all came from?"

Piper was not for turning that quickly.

"Come here sweet Pi..."

Dande's long arms outstretched, for the benefit of the audience.

"Pee-pi-po, come here. Please let me off. I'm a crazy-bitch-diva, you know that. Sorry sweetie."

"I'm not being difficult. I just don't see how I'm meant to get past it so easily."

The usually failsafe baby talk wasn't cutting it with Piper and they all saw it.

"Okay guys. Take it easy. Let's just talk it through, no one wants to go down this road."

"Actually, Suki's right. We're all friends, let's not do this. Guys, shall we leave you two to it...we'll just relocate to the lounge."

Nancy the voice of reason, determined to help them see sense.

"Good idea. A little privacy is what's needed..."

Clara agreed, holding a coffee filled bowl, headed to the next room. Despite Dande's plea to the contrary, the others followed suit.

Dande was never a fan of elephant-in-the-room scenarios. All that inner congregational conflict went against her open nature. With a penchant for filling quiet moments with her own voice, she broke the standoff.

"Piper. Can I get you anything before we start?

Lunch coming soon, though?"

"Yeah, a big fat line…" sneered Piper.

"Haha, funny…oh?"

Then Piper plundered her old Dolce tote bag, racked up a white heap onto the work surface of the island, scraping and shaping a pair of tracks. She knew full well that Dande was trying to go clean. Daytime gear was a no no these days for her…she was at the Al Anon, NA and AA every week, trying not to get on it. Piper barely tapped the residue from her credit card before holding her tussled hair to one side and speedily snaffling up the marching powder.

Her eyes prompted Dande to indulge.

"Piper…" Dande was indignant. "You know I can't do this, it's too early."

"That's not what you said last night?"

"Well, okay…halve that, then. Last night I was under pressure, as you well know."

"What's wrong with you? Sugar St Jean was a bloody long time ago. Move on. Taking it out on me - no fair!"

"So somebody tries to rip your life to shreds and you stand back, do you? I will never…NEVER…speak to that bitch again. It's okay for you, Charlie never strays."

"Look don't bring Charlie into it. What made you kick off like that? Stick to the point."

"I'm always kicking off. Doesn't have to mean anything. I'm a diva. Diva Dande. You know I blow up over nothing, but I don't hold grudges."

"You said some things last night which we're not gonna gloss over, mate."

"Like what? What?"

"You said I was in on it. I set you up. Like I'd do such a thing. Thought we were friends?"

"What? I was mad at Sugar, not you. I lashed out at you, but she was the one I was mad at really."

"I tried to calm you down, but you were like...never seen you this bad. You hate me."

"Hey, hey, hey...it's Sugar I hate. I detest her. I'm sorry for what I said. I didn't mean anything."

"I'm not letting this go just like that, D. You said I was always hanging up my phone or hiding my mobile or something. What did you mean?"

"Did I?"

"Don't fuck about. You were getting at something and I don't like it."

Dande played dumb, shrugged and leaned into Piper and whispered, "Piper, darling. I can't remember. I can't. Can we just forget about it? I want us to stay

friends. You're like my little sis. You know that. Please. Let's hug it out. Come on..."

Dande's arms outstretched for a second time, cuddling her pal. Piper's arms tightly tucked in.

Clara appeared. "Aww, that's better, guys. Just came to get the salt. Can I?"

"Really Clara?" Dande peered over Piper's shoulder.

"We're done here anyway," added Piper, "We're not getting anywhere. Can't be arsed with it anymore."

"Piper, please...we've got to work on this TV shit together. Let's not drag it out. I love you, Pi. Please. I'm sorry. See I'm saying sorry! Sorry, sorry, sorry, sorry."

The rest of the crew piled in trying to hug things out between themselves also.

"While I'm at it, sorry for my behaviour, guys. I owe you all a massive apology. I came close to messing this up for all of us. It's all about the Housewives of House. Let's make it happen," beamed Dande.

"I'm just gonna say one more thing...if it wasn't for the Housewives of House I'd be off," poo-pooed Piper.

"Don't be like that," intervened Suki. "We're a team guys. We're gorgeous and we love each other. Love 'n' light...sisterhood vibes, yeah?"

They burst out laughing in unison as Suki went all hipster on them.

"Anyway, what you gonna do about Bertie, D?"

Nancy skilfully moved the conversation on, and it was back to talking about the kids, tiredness and the drawbacks of modern parenting.

White Isle White Lies

Dande was sitting in the massive villa in Santa Eularia, Ibiza, sipping a mojito, shouting down the phone against the chillout music in the background, "What time's the flight? When do you get in?" Repeat.

As they had done since forming their friendship, the Five-Go-Hard were flying into Ibiza to spend quality 'family time' with their DJ partners. The fuss about taxis, who's picking up who and what restaurants they'd be meeting at, making sure cots had been supplied, was all part of the fun. Over a period of two or three days it would be manic communication central, until they were all settled for the next two to three weeks.

This season they were booked to stay in a newly refurbished finca turned villa...

They always kept it simple, and ate nearby or ordered in: trying to settle the children, especially when they were younger. With their tweenies and teenies, fussy eaters and insomniacs, the task was trying.

The sooner the routine was established, the sooner they could devise themselves a party rota. They all had to get on it at some point. It's Ibiza and the party never stops...children or not.

Suki took on the most babysitting duties, joined by Clara - IVF sessions permitting. She had been trying for years. While on treatment she would go 'free from', but after the negative results she would go headlong into a mild depression that only self-medicating on ecstasy, coke and a toke could lift her from.

The girls knew that the binge sessions called on by Clara were an inevitable part of her cycle that often tested their own willpowers. That girl could 'pardy' hard. She was both queen of the basement party and duchess of the rooftop, always able to lure the group with her catchphrase, "You've got to see this place."

As a result, Piper, whose daughter Poppy was of similar age to Lola Lyon, Dande's daughter, would stay out together with Nancy…until her three-year-old, Kitty was born. Hers being the youngest changed the dynamics. She hung back to babysit with Suki more often than not.

Dande's mum, Mrs Lyon, would come out to look after the kids for the 'big party'.

Every year it was different. Some huge promoter would book DJ Charlie Fenchurch for an exclusive pool party. Charlie always got his mates in on it and so it developed into a traditional line-up, with DJs Eli Stefano, Baxta Henshaw, Flemming Michaels and Razr Denzle. This was the pinnacle of their vacation. The boys either showed up to hang out with their families or were MIA with no questions, no demands. The hazard of the job on the White Isle.

Networking and hedonism was what made Ibiza tick. New players, legendary players, loud and wild, heavy and underground this playground of the lost and found, paid the bills and brought the thrills. The clear veneered line was understood by the Five-Go-Hard. So the annual trip was a formality of sorts. However, the opening and closing parties were 'no gos'. There were exceptions, when the child-free relationships were in the honeymoon period or when the DJ partner was in the dog house, and a romantic getaway was the solution. Then, the kids would stay home. A very rare occurrence.

The villa was a multiple guest open plan design, with chill out zones, sofas and day beds and an alfresco bathroom, which even had Funktion One speakers!

At the bottom end of the Moorish tiled second pool area, surrounded by foliage, was where the adults privately huddled under heated lamps and candles for that cheeky smoke or 'straightener' to delay a come down or avoid a whitey.

The kids were forbidden to go down there, which made it all the more attractive to them. One designated adult was always on lookout duty.

Had there been a hidden camera, Piper and Eli would have made their own show. Always giggling in the den, whichever villa they stayed in. It was standard. They were the comedians of the group. Piper's blog was popular because of her humour, yet in real life she only found her 'fun' in Eli's company. They were all one big family. Why would anyone read anything more into it than that? She was like a sister to Dande.

One warm evening Piper overheard that Dande was heading out while Eli was returning to the villa. Piper invented a headache and stayed back. She lived for these holidays, ever since their affair began all those years ago. When Dande, Clara and Nancy rode out of sight in a white cab, that was her signal to get changed. None of the other DJs would be about until the early hours...perhaps. So only Suki remained, who would be on her iPad in the games area...or putting finishing touches to her latest watercolour landscape in the dark, occasionally dipping her brush in her glass of sangria by mistake.

Piper could rock a cossie like no other. Fresh from her shower, hair still wet, doused in Dior oil, she went for the full costume. Cut low to her navel, and high past her hips. It was a dark bronze number with Bizanntine style embellishments, where the gold caught the light in all the right places. The matching silk sarong hung low, tied below her pubis. She waited and watched from the lounge balcony for Eli to arrive in his taxi. She hurried over as he stumbled out in shorts, a vest and open shirt.

"Eli!" She could hardly contain herself. "Fancy a night cap? Just making one."

Eli, however smashed, was going to have a drink before bed.

"Yeah, what we havin'?"

"Wait and see! Bringing it over to the little pool!"

She hoisted her boobs to exacting proportions after stirring up her little love cocktail.

"Nice!"

Eli's nonchalant response was for pure effect. He recognised that tone in Piper's voice. He told himself to knock her back gently and mean it this time. In haste he fastened up his shirt lopsidedly. He could hear her Jimmy Choo flip flops slapping down the pathway. The solar light sensors flickered as the figure strolled leisurely towards him to a fanfare of ice clinking against the hi-ball glass under the golden light. Here she was, the petite princess to his Amazonian goddess, Dande. Glistening tanned skin, beach hair, smelling like paradise. His eyes followed the lines of the low-cut halter neck as it crossed her décolletage snugly over the curve of her bosom, her navel winking at him through the peephole detail.

She leant over so that she could maximise the impact of her upper body. Her thigh gap jutting out through the sarong, revealing the thong where it barely strapped her neatly waxed mound, he was now so desperate to enter.

Piper's work was done. Eli's was a groin easily stirred. She playfully looked down at herself as she handed him the mojito with a twist.

"Oh, this cossie is a size too small, haha... My bits are in agony...let me just..."

Piper used her free hand to slide the gusset, fingering herself for a few seconds before dipping both her middle and ring fingers in her drink and licking them.

Eli leaned back, wanting to scan the area, but his gaze was transfixed on the vixen and her sticky digits. She stirred his drink with her fingers and stuck it in his mouth before lunging in for a rambunctious kiss. Deep and cold, slow and laboured, her tongue devoured his.

The biting point at which Eli went from passive to passion was almost magical. It was sudden and ferocious. He took over proceedings. His huge biceps gripped Piper's waist as he hoisted her towards him and bent her over against the nearby giant galvanised zinc planter. Her shellacs hit the decks, scratched to fuck...to fuck.

Her hair caught in the bushes as she turned her head sideways in the soil, Eli made swift moves, holding her in place with one hand and sliding off his shorts with the other. As he lowered himself untangling his feet, he pressed his mouth into her from behind, licking her ready for him. They would have to be quick. She moaned softly and deeply, writhing her pelvis in absolute divine ecstasy. She widened her buttock cheeks so the cool air wafted within her. When she thought he was about to trace another lap with his tongue, she felt the girth of him pushing into her so hard she cried out. He yanked her hair as she bit her fist in an effort to keep quiet. But Eli had to hit that pussy, nothing seemed more urgent than ramming her. This was pleasure he wanted more pace with. She felt amazing against him. Her clit banging against the metal with his solid thrusts. He kissed the nape of her neck gently, then tilted her. One leg splayed, he was making her pussy scissor clamp his rod. At the point his ardour took over he slammed in and out of her like a machine. They came seconds after, slowly, breathlessly drawing themselves out of each other. Sweat and sex dripped from them as they got their garms together. Slurping their drinks, steadily adjusting themselves, they giggled.

"Well, good evening Mr Stefano."

"What a welcome!" panted Eli.

"Will sir be staying on? You put in quite a performance."

"Sir will be staying turned on. The finger licking, though, was quite unnecessary."

"I'll use just the one finger next time, eh?"

"Jesus! Don't set me off again."

"Why not? You want it, don't you?"

"Haha, seriously, Pi, we can't keep doing this. I love it. I love you, but if we get..."

"We won't. Stop panicking, Elijah! We'll work something out. You can't deny the connection."

"It's electric. I feel the same way too. But I'm not leaving Dande. Why do you make me have to say that?"

"Hush, let's just enjoy the moment. When can we next...?"

"Babe, come sit next to me. Let's see how it goes. If we can, great. If we can't we'll have to wait until we get back."

Eli snuggled her into his chest and kissed the top of her head. This post coital affection made her love him all the more.

Charlie would have gone straight into the shower. The intimacy between them had depleted to the occasional hand job. He was in denial about losing her. He provided her and the kids with a comfortable life. He was absolute in opinion that she would never find anyone else as devoted as he was to her. If he had been a woman, he was convinced that he had landed on his feet with him. To some extent he was right. Her walk-in closet, her beauty products and endless spa days kept a buoyancy in place as they drifted along weathering the calm and storm of domesticity that had been once a shore thing.

Piper's connection with Eli was not about money. She was unaware that she was entering a period of transformation, where her values and needs had changed. She had only just begun to recognise the power of sharing deepest emotional thoughts with a lover. Having someone willing to listen, be equally kind, funny and attentive was what she craved now. Eli was generally unavailable, which sowed the seeds of early onset obsession over the unattainable. The kind where any excuse to talk about him or any amusing or any anecdotal stories was saved and honed and considered, before sharing with him...to him...for him.

While making the kids tea or having a mani-pedi, her thoughts turned to him. Even her vague interest in music production came into its own just to keep up with Eli's ambitions. Ironically, she never paid much attention to the doings in the basement studio of their three-story townhouse. DJ Charlie Fenchurch was the man-of-the-moment with his 'Fenners Faderz Remix' series. It just simply went over her head.

It was all about Eli and what he liked to eat, travel, dance to, what sport he enjoyed, his child-hood...and she even empathised about his son's situation, Amy and her addictions. She wondered day after day about sexy underwear, her hair and what clothes Eli liked to see her in. She was the shining beacon of DJ WAGs: Housewives of Houses every-where. Beautiful, petite, stylish and had bagged a top jock...or two. She was aware of her own status, yet as uncomfortable with it as she was, she also rev-eled in it. Not so anymore.

Initially, lust was the factor that drew them to-gether. Piper being the social networker used her skills to manipulate their secret meet ups.

She would scribble a piece for her blog in one hour, then spend the rest of her time staking out DJ Eli Stefano gigs online. She would trawl through past gigs looking at photos of the female fans on various feeds. Spotting faces of the usual subjects posturing, pawing and pouting over her lover. New faces really bugged her. Who were they? What did they do? Would he give up Dande for one of them, even?

Piper was like a stubborn staple you tried to pull off a centrefold. She wanted to know his every move in order to coordinate their rendezvous. He never seemed to be on top of his pending dates. Eli was oblivious to her acute knowledge of his bookings. She had masterminded almost all of their times together. She knew Dande's movements, which made planning less complicated. The guilt-gilded affair became far less so after a few years. All Eli had to do was turn up. He had never knowingly turned down a hook up. Piper was no exception.

Worst of all Piper was fully versed in the ardent fervour of her lover. He was a player. His pretty boy Mauritian features and 6'4" frame saw to that. She was determined that once he committed to her, his penchant for groupies would be a thing of the past. She knew what made them tick…she had been one, once upon a time.

*****

The biggest night of the group's Ibiza season was looming. The Five-Go-Hard always insisted on going out for a last-minute rabble-rousing shopping spree for the big night. It was more of an excuse for a cocktail tour de force that threatened to ruin them prior to the main event. Dande's mum would fly in for the babysitting honours. The relief on her arrival was palpable. At last they could kick up their heels without reprise. Mrs Lyon, not quite five feet, made motherhood look easy. In contrast to her relationship with her own daughter that was left wanting, according to Dande, at least. Her issues and AA meetings hinged on these unresolved matters.

The guys were in and out of the villa all hours, smoking or getting on it by the little pool. They struggled with phone signals and could be seen wandering the grounds like wildebeests on the plain. DJ Flemming Michaels was the most considerate, looking in on "Mrs L" once in a while to make sure she wasn't overstretching herself with the kids.

Eli's son Bertie was nearly 14 and impatient with the younger ones. Piper's boy, ten-year-old Luke would attempt to keep him occupied, but the age gap just made him hugely annoying. Bertie had slyly sussed out the wifi strength there and had ordered extra data for his gadgets. Point blank refusing to let everyone in on the exact spot where the signal was strongest. In this secret spot he sat by himself hour after hour only, turning up for lunch or dinner and his regular order of burger and fries. The persistent nagging from the adults, especially the males who thought they were 'down with da kids', irritated the life out of him. The group tried to sympathise with Dande about Bertie, but were unconvincing.

The day of the big party arrived and some of the group were pushing on through after an impromptu sit up by the small pool when Charlie returned to the villa with US superstar DJ Ernie Hernandez and a couple of his cronies. Ernie was on the island for his annual raft of Ibiza bookings. He nodded at the group in various states of sobriety.

Unusually, some ketamine was being passed around. When the kids were about as a rule they stuck to coke and tokes. They had all indulged and monged out in different spells over the course of the early hours. Nancy, Clara, Suki, Piper and Dande bonded by their inability to communicate on this level. Giggling, not laughing, speaking, not saying, staring, not seeing anything in particular. This heavy sesh was a whole evening early. In a bid to straighten up, they felt they had no choice but to indulge in copious measures of coke as they cracked on.

This included lunching with the kids. Pretending to eat. Drinking Lemsips. Nipping off for little disco naps before the children dragged them outside again.

The pizzas made them wretch, but it was the easiest thing to cook. Mrs L was oblivious. From what she could tell they were a bunch of hungover parents who "meant well" on the whole. They were at the mercy of her daughter, Dande, whom she considered the ringleader.

Four cabs arrived. The music was blaring and the villa was alive with sounds echoing through the woods nearby. The kids were hyper, picking up on their parents in party mode.

Their sparkly mums in variations of designer white ensemble from Helmut Lang, Joseph, Isabel Marant, Missoni, Balmain and Maison Margiela...in georgette or cotton twills, silks and other amazing fabric. Sparkly 'fun' makeup, espadrilles wedges, earrings swinging in their restlessness, as they danced about between the lounge and patio area.

The children were dressed for bed but allowed to stay up until they left. Collectively the parents accepted that their sprogs picked up their energy from them, demanding and asking for things impossible to agree on at that time of night.

Poppy had a habit of tapping Piper's elbow.

"Mummy, can we go Disneyland Paris tomorrow?"

"No darling, we're on holiday in Spain. Daddy will take you half term," reasoned Piper, calmly appeasing her daughter, while waiting for the next question.

"Can I get my nails painted like Lola's?"

"Pops? Really? Right now?"

Suki to the rescue.

"I'll do them quickly for you now if mum says it's okay,"

"We're leaving in a minute, Suki."

"I don't mind."

"They won't dry, she'll only get it everywhere and..." Piper looked round at her cute child and said: "...you bite your nails anyway. Until you stop..."

Poppy turned in her arms limply in front of her, stomping over to her dad, Charlie.

He stroked her chin while she clutched to his waist as he carried on chatting with the lads.

At a break in the convo he looked down at her and asked: "You alright, Peanut?"

"No, Mummy won't let me paint my nails like Lola's."

"Never mind. One day, when you're older..."

"But Lola's only six and I'm nine. It's not fair. Auntie Dande let's Lola do everything I can't. Wish she was my mum."

Charlie ignored her squeaky rants and carried on with the boys...about the sets they would be playing later.

Lola was being chased in a game of tag by Luke, laughing hysterically at her shrill screams as he turned himself into a monster. They ran amok, knocking over drinks, jumping over the sofas and messing up the plants outside the patio. Being shouted at by parent after parent and Nanna Lyon.

"Lola! Slow down, put some shoes on outside," rapped Dande.

"Luke!"

A stern face from Piper didn't cut it.

"Lola, dumpling...go put your flip flops on...no running!"

Eli's softly approach sometimes worked, not always.

"Watch it Luke... careful boy," disciplined Charlie halfheartedly.

Bertie was gaming in his hideout. Away from the madness.

"Come on kids. Calm down, you'll wake up Kitty. Why don't we have some ice cream?" bribed Mrs Lyon.

"Nanna, Nanna. He's gonna get me, argh!"

The shrill screaming followed, stopping everyone in their tracks. The kids could not be coaxed into the kitchen. As per usual they wanted to be with their parents.

Nanna Lyon's offer would mean ice cream, teeth brushed and then bed. They wanted to be part of the social excitement.

*****

The night was balmy. The full moon lit the sky. The parade of hugs, kisses and hi-fives played out as three taxis arrived.

Charlie, Eli and Dande always bagsied the front seats being the giants of the group.

Piper hung back to see which cab Eli was getting in and joined him with Clara.

Which left Nancy and Suki in Dande's cab. DJ Razr Denzle sat behind Charlie in the all-boys cab, next to DJs Flemming Michaels and Baxta Henshaw.

As their cab took off, Piper leaned forward clutching the front seat, rubbing Eli's shoulders in the friendly non-threatening way she always did. The banter rolled on, as their comedy taxi driver told well-worn tales of the supermodels he had picked up over the years, in broken Spanglish. They cracked up he drove recklessly on the corners providing ample excuses for Piper to hold on to the shoulders of her secret lover's white shirt.

That over-enthused expression of mirth, the ritual a woman in love does to attract her mate, was in full effect as Piper, away from Dande's gaze, flopped around Eli like a rag doll on acid. Eli felt a little uneasy by it. Clara didn't pay the slightest bit of notice. They were all off their heads, flying by the seat of their pants to push on through the evening.

*****

The convoy of white taxis bobbed and weaved over rocky, dirt tracks with full beams on lighting the way, the odd silvery moth flickering across the windscreens. As they got closer the distant music boomed across the landscape. Dazzling blue and white LED lights swirled up to a clearing, where more cars and 4x4s started to arrive from all directions. The electricity in the air was intense. The crowd were mainly wearing white, some fully clothed and others dared to bare. The floodlit giant projection bounced a 'welcome' sign to the guests and the stilt artists showered glitter confetti.

It was all a bit much for the west Londoner's more subtle taste, but they made an exception for Charlie's mate, Fronton, who was an over the top metrosexual events organiser and promoter. His private parties were legendary, and his August birthday bash was not to be missed. He would seek out unique isolated spaces from fincas to warehouses, remote bays and secluded state-of-the-art cliffside villas. His high-end marquee hire concepts, always wowed his well-heeled international guests.

As each of them got out the car the response as they gazed skywards was the same.

"Wow!"

The girls hugged and squealed at each other in anticipation of the messy night to come. Any sluggishness from the last 24 hours was eroded by the sheer theatre of the night kicking in a second wind.

"Oh. My. God! This is unbelievable," cried out Nancy.

"Oh my dayz, as Bertie would say."

"Holy, fuckin' shit. This is nuts," exclaimed Razr.

"How does he do it? Like - every time!"

Eli stood back shaking his head.

"I think I'm coming up and I haven't done anything for ages…haha."

Clara held her head.

"Don't think I'll ever sleep again! Should've worn me shades!"

Suki also held her head.

Charlie beckoned them on.

"Let's go find the man."

Charlie winked at Piper, but she pretended not to see, conveniently fixing the back of her shorts. Then she skipped closer to him and grabbed his hand as he expected her to walk in with him. DJ Charlie Fenchurch's wife, no less had to step up.

It had become a bit tedious, strutting her stuff, giving it the biggun' in a bid to ward off wannabe DJ WAGs: Housewives of Houses skanking about when she actually couldn't care less if he left her.

Charlie, for all their relationship woes, still loved having Piper on his arm. Her bronzed iridescent body butter finish on her arms, chest and legs gave her an ethereal glow. Crowned by her loose top knot, she reigned on style. Delicately holding her cross body, Chlöe 'Drew' bag, she focused straight ahead, like Kate Moss on the catwalk, model stare with each step. The attention from their fellow VIP guests was indeed for headliner Charlie. But the other females were watching her closely, or so she thought. In reality they were mostly too off their own heads to give a damn.

Dande and Suki were arm in arm, their fellas Eli and Razr hands over shoulders. Clara and DJ Flemming Michaels walked in together single file holding hands, while Nancy and DJ Baxta Henshaw also held each other close as they strolled in.

A procession of waving to old faces and winced smiles at randoms as they dance-shuffled through the throng, deep house mixes chugging away.

From nowhere a six-foot, platinum blonde model, reached out.

"Shaaarlaaay, you're 'ere! Mmmwah. Fronton says he'll be down to see you soon. But first, guys, come with me."

She ushered them in her French twang, greeting Charlie with three side kisses…ignoring Piper altogether. A path was cleared to make way for the headline DJ to try and reach the main room, but this was a struggle. Each room they passed, through the heaving crowds, had vintage circus big top themed décor as its backdrop.

And real animals…there were real animals! So un-PC, but white powdered elephants, a white tiger on a leash and white horses circled a huge white merry-go-round… The illusion between fixed objects and moving animals fooled their senses. Each room filled with the hue of either blue or pink LED lights. Totally surreal and the all white masked trapeze waiters and clowns, all dressed in white from hair, face paint to the usually red nose, white on white stripy suits and giant shoes. Instructed to scare the party-goers senseless.

At last they got to their plot for the night, to an area behind the main decks, a waiter on hand at a pop-up bar exclusively for them. They were surprised to see International giant, Jett Setter playing on the CDJs. They got tanked up on the usual generous spirit measures poured on the White Isle, and particularly to VIPs. Once settled, Clara squeezed Es into everybody's palms.

"Ah, shit and shit and fucking shit," yelled an exasperated Eli, bashing his head with his fist.

"What, what?" said Piper.

"Left my vinyl back at the villa, haven't I?"

"You idiot," snapped Charlie. "We've all got ours. How did you manage that?"

"I'll have to go back. Our new mixes are in there. Jake's coming, I could get him to pick them up on his way."

"Where's he staying again?"

"Near San An he said. Fuck sake, man!"

Eli was turning around on the spot in frustration.

Dande chipped in. "You can't go all the way back? You'll just have to make do. I'm sure the guys have got some spare music, right?"

If looks could kill, Dande was dead twice over. Eli was not in the mood.

"Butt out D!"

"You what?"

Nancy consoled Dande and swerved her away from the tension brewing.

Piper smirked, but Charlie nudged her firmly. "Cut it out."

"For fuck sake. I can't get a signal here. Shit. Look Charlie, I'm gonna see if I can pick up a signal outside. If not, I'm heading straight for the villa."

"Is he going?" Dande could just make out Eli's unmistakably broad shoulders, his open shirt flying behind him.

"Leave him to it, Dande. By the time the others have played he'll be back for his part of the set."

Nancy the voice of reason prevailed again. Backed up by Suki.

"Yeah...he'll be alright, D. Let's do some shots."

"Hmmm, it is a buzz killer."

"Only if we let it!"

"Somebody say shots? Ahaha!" enthused Clara

"In," agreed Nancy.

"Where's Piper?" asked Dande. "She was here just a second ago."

Just picking up on this chat, Charlie butted in. "She's just nipped out to the loo…or for a fag…or something."

The rest of the lads focused on the job they had ahead of them. Eli's fuck-up had thrown them a little. Letting Fronton down was not an option. Charlie was in work mode and his single-minded diligence was about the gig. Piper's welfare took a back seat.

What was an amazing spectacle on entry became an annoying obstacle course when Eli tried to leave. He kept tapping his mobile hoping the 'no signal' sign would turn into two bars, hopefully three. He was so anxious he didn't spot Piper trying to keep up with him. At last they were at the clearing. Piper tugged his short sleeves.

"Hey, try my phone," she said, her kind, love-struck eyes glistening in LED light reflection.

"Pi? Oh? Okay. Thanks. Can you tap Jake's number in for me."

"Yes, read it out. Wait a second…okay." A calming port in a storm was Piper, in situations that Dande would over-dramatise. Eli was beginning to appreciate this. She dialled the number and handed it over.

"Argghh! Still can't get through. It's just ringing." Eli's frustration was rising again.

"Give it here, babe. Let me text him for you."

As she did it she read out what she wrote…

Mate. Left record boxes at the villa. The one by

the windmill. Please pick up on your way a.s.a.p. Mrs L is there. In new flight cases. PS...my phone no signal. Using Piper's. Eli.

"Great. Thank you. Press send quick. Quick!"

"Done. It's done."

"Let's wait until he responds. Give it five or so minutes. Man, this is unbearable!"

"I'm gonna have this fag. D'ya mind?"

"Nah, go ahead."

Piper lit up, brushing the ashes from her nipples as they fell under the spaghetti strapped pearlescent top, inwardly so pleased with herself that she had been mentioned in dispatches in the message to Jake. Even if she did write it herself.

"Ahhh! This top's new. Look at it. Fucking ash all over it," she added, styling out her smugness.

"You look great Piper. Has he messaged you yet?"

Piper's heart flipped somersaults enough for an Olympic gymnast.

"Let me just check...and yes! Blessim. Message says...

You fuckwit. I will turn cab round and get them at villa. Who will be up? And can you take cab to nearest landmark so that they will direct my driver to Fronton's place. My driver doesn't know it.

"Let me see, Piper. Give it to me."

Eli was drunk, but he had to see this message for himself and reply...

Thank you!!!

"Sorry, Pi. Thanks for helping. Come with me in a

cab down the road to pick up Jake?"

"What right now? Jake's nowhere near yet and we've only just got here ourselves…"

"Babe, no worries. Go back in. Thanks for the phone. Come back out when Jake texts again please."

"No, no, I don't mind waiting with you. Err, shall we go for a little stroll away from these lights?"

"Erm, dunno. What if someone sees us? We need the signal," she hesitated.

"We're only going for a walk to get a better signal on my phone? So I'm having to go with you?"

"You crafty bitch, Jake won't be here for an hour," winked Eli.

They kept an obvious gap between them as they left silently, into the woods, the party lights on the horizon.

"So you've got a new track, then?"

"Let's change the subject, I'm so pissed off with myself."

"I think my pill is kicking in…"

"Didn't take mine yet. Not before my set. If it wasn't Fronton's gig, probably would've already."

Eli started rustling something out of his buttoned shorts, coins pocket.

"What you doing? Haha…need help?"

"Actually yeah. See if you can get that little pouch out, can't seem to undo it."

"Let me have a look."

Piper shone her phone torch on it.

"My nails are getting stuck. You're best taking them off. Haha… What's in there?"

"What do you think? Let's have a little livener. That'll straighten you out a bit. Need you compos mentis for the texts…"

Eli unzipped his flies, leant against a tree piling

the powder on his thumb before snorting. He offered Piper, who did the same.

"Ah that's better!"

Eli with his dangling manhood. Those shorts demanded commando. Piper was determined to make it grow. She sat down provocatively to remove her wedges which were ragingly uncomfortable during the woodland walk.

As she stood up they locked eyes. He dived into her mouth, the bitter taste of coke in their throats, their tongues in need of the other grappled, subsided and roamed.

Eli's huge body pressed up against her on the tree. His hardness evident as he stooped to hers. She traced his firm, hirsute curve as it rose and he responded with the moans she longed to hear.

All at once he dropped to his knees and reached under the flaps of her shorts with his fore fingers and buried his tongue in her, the way she always liked it. She raised her arms clutching the back of the tree almost in yoga salutation pose and writhed as he flicked and licked, alternating the pressure between hard and soft. She looked up at the stars to the barely lit leaves and branches. She let herself feel him.

Fingers, teeth, tongue exquisitely in motion, the sweet textures were too delicious to succumb to the ecstasy of it or hold back for the main event. But it was futile as he worked inside her. She burst as he sucked her clit like a straw. She bucked, repeatedly crying out as she grabbed his hair, then quivered on the dry grassland.

"Ahh. Oh my god...ahh...ahhhhhh...ahh."

Piper tried to restore herself.

They chuckled together. He, now sat, legs spread,

back against the tree. He was still at full attention. Grinning away at the splendour of himself. Piper knew what she had to do and stalked on all fours towards him. She gripped his rod between her palms, caressing him up and down before sliding the whole head in her mouth and out again. Contorting her head and neck to accommodate the whole of him down her throat, salivating as she did so, slurping rhythmically as she got into her stride. He painfully yanked her head, almost ruining her top knot for a feral kiss and then shoved her back on the job. She kept the pace.

He cried out "Piper...fuck...ahh...ahhhhhhhhhh!"

It was his turn to slump and quiver breathlessly.

"What have you done to me you dirty bitch?"

"What have you done to me you fucking bastard?"

They embraced, before checking the phone.

"What am I gonna do about you, Pi?"

"I dunno, but I love you, E..."

Eli jumped to his feet pulled her up and insisted they head back, whatever. Searching for his shorts and the gear, which they finished on the way back.

The distraction was just what Eli needed, but when they got closer to the site, they noticed they were covered in Ibizan's characteristic, red soil. They looked a sight.

Facing each other, they panicked about getting their stories straight. This would be the closest they had come in years to getting found out.

"Okay. So I followed you to get a signal. I slipped and fell down a slope and you got dirty trying to pick me up?"

"Not far from the truth. Look at us though?"

"Well it could happen. Say the pills were too

strong and I lost it a little."

"Hmmm, who'd believe that? Let's say we got striped up? Say somebody gave us Keta-Coke or something?"

"Yeah, that'll work! Fucking hell. Look at us. Freaking 'white' party. Hang on…"

"What? You got a text?"

"Let me look…yes, it's from Jake! He's got the flight cases. Is 10 mins away. Get a cab to meet his cab outside Gardenias?"

"Yes. I know it. Coming?

"May as well, I'm here now."

They jumped in one of the many cabs dropping people off. Snogging all the way there. Piper took advantage of Eli's good mood, now buzzing with relief.

Jake was greeted emphatically by the two adult urchins as he got in the front seat, flight cases safely locked in the boot.

"What the fuck happened to you two? Did a hedge run into you or summink?"

"Something like that…haha. Fell down trying to get a signal" tried Piper.

"More like 'hedging' your bets someone's gonna believe ya! Ha-ha…"

"Smart arse!"

Eli almost gave the game away.

"How'd you manage to leave the boxes, mate? They're the new ones!"

"I don't know. It's Ibiza, innit? Always drama. Thanks though mate. What a palaver!"

"What's it like down there, buddy?"

"It's buzzing…heaving. You'll see in a sec!"

The cab swung round and stopped at the drop-off point.

"Oh my dayz! It's like the aliens have landed!" exclaimed Jake on arrival.

Piper opted to linger sheepishly, a couple of steps behind the boys, already being patted on their backs as they carried their boxes through.

Finally they joined the rest of their party. Celebratory ebullience from the lads and the women quizzical, but under very, very wasted conditions, everybody was already too smashed to pick up on Piper's bedraggled appearance. The magic of it was, that the red dirt was invisible to the naked eye, bleached out by the speciality light works.

Piper explained her version of what had happened, but couldn't hold anyone's interest. Least of all Dande, whose grimace said it all. It was all about getting more and more trashed. And that, they did.

Eli took his shirt off to play his set, which went down well. He played Piper's favourite tune 'Fall For You' by Kings of Tomorrow (feat April). She immediately took centre stage in the VIP and rocked that tune out with all she had, jumping, shaking her head, hands in the air, drink in hand, bag flying...singing her lungs out.

Would it be wrong if I fall for you?

The party turnt-up to the max, the Five-Go-Hard jumped on Piper's infectious vibe,

The headliner DJ, Charlie Fenchurch was now in the house and all set to smash it. He fired up a tune that set the place alight. The ravers couldn't get enough. That was the moment Fronton showed up in his silver chrome finish vest and shorts, camping it up, as only he could. His corporate haircut at odds with his outfit despite donning a silver pirate scarf.

He was punching the air with everything he had too. He was a super fan.

The party went on all morning, and with their every whim catered for in the various rooms, from foot spas to massage chairs and imaginative chill out spaces. Even tapas canapés, when the sun came up, and they began to come down. It was a pleasure-dome of the senses.

Pilot Brainstorming (cont)

"Erm, Gillian, I was thinking that maybe we could have one or two of the ladies view it. Just feel it out, kind of?" suggested Edna gingerly.

Everyone scoffed at this ludicrous idea.

"Ain't gonna happen, Edna," sneered Dorrit.

"It's just a rough edit, though."

"Laura, what exactly isn't gelling chemistry-wise?" asked Gillian.

"Well considering Piper and Dande are meant to be best friends in it, somehow it never came across, hence when they fell out you didn't care."

"Well I never saw that. Anyone else pick this up?"

"I'm too close to it," said Edna. "I know they are or were best friends after hanging out with them a few times."

"Like I said," persisted Gillian. "We have something here. Jot over some working titles."

"I think so…" agreed Edna.

"Where are they all now…the ladies?"

"I think they're still out in Ibiza…must be due back soon, though."

"Why didn't we shoot them over there?"

Gillian was really put out at this glaring omission.

"Isn't that what it's all about? The show needed to climax out there!"

"The timing and logistics meant we couldn't do it

when they were heading out if we wanted the pilot ready for now. We could have cheated it. We should have. Okay. That's done then for next year…if we get the series."

"Probably, that is what's needed. We used the product launch party as the storyline vehicle, as with other shows, we need a different take on it. It needs it's own set of rules, a series about WAGs but not in a way ever seen or focused on, before and after Ibiza," enthused Edna.

"You're right. We didn't think outside the box. The setting was all wrong."

"Still don't see the characters working I'm afraid," barked Laura.

"Surely you don't have to be into house music to want to know what DJ Charlie Fenchurch's wife gets up to?"

"Like I said," interjected Polly. "We need more of the DJ's presence."

Emilee crashed in again, with the special coffee. A much needed break before Gillian had to leave again.

"Sorry, have to dash to my four o'clock in Marylebone. Let me leave you with this. I have a strong feeling we will get this commissioned. It is just a matter of refreshing our approach in making the full the series. Catch you all on…is it next Monday Charlotte?"

"Yes. Just me, you, Edna, Dorrit and Laura."

"Get Marcus to sit in as well."

"Get me in where?"

The six foot blue-suited, silver fox appeared, carrying his briefcase. Gillian beamed and clutched his shoulders as she kissed him on both cheeks.

"Ah, Marcus. Where were you? I'm just off now. Come, let's walk and talk. Bye everyone."

At this Marcus peered into the meeting group and casually waved, following Gillian out of the building.

"Well, it seems guys, that Gillian is all over it!" beamed Charlotte. "Yay! We might just have a commission, after all. But it means we have got our work cut out going forward. We'll have a helluva lot more development work to do. In the meantime, let's get our heads together. Fire over any ideas, however leftfield. Edna, you and Laura sort out how to make the talent - inverted commas - gel with each other. We need to sound them out a little. What makes them tick, what makes them laugh and dig out their worst fears. You know the drill. If Gillian likes them as is, we're going to have to flesh them out."

"Okay. I can arrange to meet up with them next week. Shall we get a meet in first Laura?"

"Yup. Haven't seen them since we wrapped."

"Bet their Ibiza trip has been fun and games. Wonder if they made up?" chimed in Polly.

"We did miss a trick there, though. Imagine shooting on location in Ibiza."

D-Day

Edna was waiting at her dental hygienist reception, phone in hand making a few work related calls.

"Piper. Darling. How are you? How was Ibiza?"

"Oh hi, Edna. All good, thanks. Got back maybe two weeks or so, I think. Could be longer. What have we missed?"

"You know. Same 'ole. Listen, just a quickie. Could you round up the girls for a meet this week? We've put something together and we've been getting some really positive feedback."

"Really? Haha! Sounds exciting. What shall we do, meet at the production office or...?"

"Actually, do you think we could do it at Dande's place...would she be up for that?"

"Erm, yeah. I'm sure she would. Let me get back to you."

"Brilliant thanks. Any time this week, day or evening. We must meet by end of the week though."

Piper sent the bulletin via their Five-Go-Hard WhatsApp group. Dande was the first to breathe a sigh of relief. They agreed Thursday evening would be best.

"Eli!"

Dande was straight on the phone to him.

"Elijah! I think we might get the show. It's happening! Piper just got a call from Edna and we're all meeting at our place on Thursday. Whoop, whoop!"

"Nice one…you deserve it. You all deserve it…but is the world ready for you guys?"

"I can't believe it myself. You playing out Thursday?"

"Yup, as per… get the childminder in so you can relax."

"What about Bert?"

"Hmmm. I dunno. I really need to spend more time with the lad. One of us has got to get through to him."

"Anyway…great news, isn't it? I'll make an extra special family dinner tonight. Sooo happy. Love you."

"Love you too! Well done!"

For the rest of that week every conversation was dominated by talk of whether they really would get a TV series.

The joy of anticipation of what this reality show could mean for them and where it could lead even gave Dande and Piper reason to bury their grudge for the greater good.

The Five-Go-hard had not been back to Dande's since that sushi lunch. But they had hung out at a couple of birthday celebrations for the kids and one of the DJs, which was lunch at The Whippet, Kensal Rise or in Suki's minimal kitchen for Razr's birthday drinks…or tea and cake at Nancy's.

In preparation for the big day, and ever conscious of keeping their heads clear, the girls booked themselves in for a spa day on the Wednesday in Surrey using Charlie's Addison Lee account to drive them down there. They used every bit of talk time on the subject.

"On some of these shows they get to go to some amazing spas, you know."

"I know, I've been watching them all back to back ever since…"

"Me too…they go away on nice trips as well!"

"Yes, in private frickin' jets. Oh my God…can you just imagine it?"

"Stop. Stop. I can't cope with the excitement. I can't…"

"Well, we don't wanna come over as crass. Some of these women have no style at all. Seriously provincial."

"I think vintage and Boho are swear words on most of these shows. Thank God for Reena. I don't get why they want us? I'm not complaining, though."

"Yes, they go for obvious labels. Emerging designers and retro means nothing to them…and everything to us. We mustn't lose who we are whatever happens."

"These TV people will have a darn good go, though. I don't actually trust them."

"It's not enough to be on telly. Social media, Instagram and stuff plays a part."

"Fuck sake, Piper. Don't scare us before we've even begun."

"Haha, I'm not. Just let's be realistic. There's usually an agenda at play somewhere."

"I know, but I'm up for being sponsored by designers. I'll wear anything they throw at me," said Nancy.

They collapsed into fits of laughter. When they got to their suite, donning their towelling robes, Clara produced some coke, for a "cheeky" boost. It was most welcome. All this health kick had hit their crave buttons. The bottle of bubbly DJ Flemming Michaels had ordered ahead for them was a lovely touch.

* * * * *

Back at the production office Thursday morning, Edna was sitting in on a conference call from Gillian to the team, who was at a TV conference in Nice.

Before Gillian was put through Edna looked at a row of glum faces.

"It must be urgent to call this meeting from France. Do you think she has secured the commission?"

"Well, it seems to have reached the top of her agenda."

"Yes. I noticed the group emails."

"I think we've worked out the winning formula for the show," Laura Cave, the Casting Producer, firmly asserted.

Edna felt a knot in her stomach.

"Hellooo guys. I have news."

Gillian proceeded to explain how she had managed to secure the series commission. They had to wait until the ink dried on the final decision in October. Standard procedure. But it meant they all had a job on again. A uniquely formatted show that would set tongues wagging and that had the potential to run and run.

"So we've been given the green light," continued Gillian. "Unfortunately, we won't be airing the pilot, and we will be revising the show and bringing in the concept team to firm up the format. We're going with a provisional working title for now. We like the Housewives of House. I've briefed Laura in more detail so I'll leave her to explain. I must dash. Well done all...we've got ourselves a show."

The meeting room was filled with claps and cheers.

"Okay, settle down…we haven't got much time here," said Charlotte raising her tone. "But a new commission is great news for the company," she added, to assure the freelancers.

"Yay!" interrupted Edna, now a single clapper.

"Laura, do you want to explain Gillian's points?"

"Yes. Congratulations again everyone."

Laura made eye contact with everybody around the table.

"As you know, we knew we had something special with The Housewives of House, but struggled to find the 'wow factor'. We assembled a focus group and Dande was found most unlikeable and…well… un-relatable."

"Whaaat?" shrieked Edna.

"I know. It's not easy for me to say this. As we know the group is centred around Dande, but after further viewings we thought Piper was the strongest character and the others would work seamlessly around her. We also found, sadly, that Dande just isn't TV friendly. She came across as a bit jazz handsy, a bit acty, Disney-esque…she just wasn't convincing. We will have to drop her I'm afraid."

"Laura, please, are you sure?" said Edna, in desperation. "Was it the drug references…or the argument? I mean, isn't that what we want? Larger than life characters, because she is that…"

"Sorry, Edna. The decision's been made. It's not as simple as sitting here explaining. Gillian's going on feedback and this is what they plan on doing. I am sorry. I know you have been getting to know the girls, sorry, the ladies."

"Look, is this final? I am meant to be meeting them tonight."

"That's why Charlotte asked you, so that we can

get them to agree verbally in principal."

Edna looked quizzically at Charlotte. "Am I meant to deliver this news to them? What if they back Dande and refuse to do it?"

"I think they know they want to do it. If not, we'll audition some new people. DJ WAGs are ten a penny. Don't worry, they won't pass this up."

"You getting soft, Edna?" added Dorrit.

"We have to be honest Edna. Dande is a bit of a diva, bringing her own stylist to the shoot? It really offended Sofia. It was totally unprofessional."

Edna slumped her head on the table, anxious by what lay ahead of her.

* * * * *

Dande was flying around sprucing her home with house music blaring. The bass on full blast. Singing the top lines, she actually had some good lungs on her. She was really going for Barbara Tucker's I Get Lifted.

"See ya, Mum, I'm out!"

Bertie trundled down the stairs, slamming the door hard. The door-knocker ricocheting was her clue that the teenager had escaped his dungeon.

"Ber-tie! Bertie-yah!"

Dande called out to him in vain. She was fuming. He had simply vanished down the road. Again.

"How does he do that?" she said under her breath.

Eli had promised to do something about the boy, but it was all talk as usual. She couldn't ignore it for much longer. He was still a minor. She had to face that she had lost control of the situation. She turned off the music with the remote and called Eli.

He didn't pick up. She sent a ranting voice message via WhatsApp.

You never fucking pick up when I need you. Bertie has run off again. I don't know where or why. I can't fucking do this on my own anymore, Eli. I just can't. God knows what he's up to? I'm so fucking worried... why aren't you?!

As 'parents' it was clear they were rapidly getting out of their depth.

* * * * *

Clara and Nancy piled into Suki's Jeep Wrangler together, bubbly in hand. Clara brought a couple of grams, just in case, of course.

"Listen guys, got us a sneaky mini pack. It might come in handy. But not in front of TV Edna...hehehe."

"What are you like? Pardy Clara," exclaimed Suki.

"It is still a school night you know? I've got a three year old," chipped in Nancy.

"Then don't partake, Mother Superior. I'm child free, so more for me!"

"Oh, sorry, Clara," followed Nancy quickly. "Didn't mean anything by that..."

"I know, I know, silly."

"Actually, when's your next IVF?" asked Suki.

"Not sure, hun. Just waiting for Flemming's mum to get through chemo. Think he's had enough of hospitals."

The conversation had suddenly taken a sombre turn. Suzi's Jeep was noisy and filled the silent space.

"Why don't you have any music in this jalopy yet, missus?"

"It's Razr's fault. He did something to it...and it hasn't worked since.

"Suki, it's been a couple of years...hahahaha."

Nancy couldn't help another baby reference, "Kitty was about 18 months when it went down..."

Nancy bit her lip. She was conscious she may have turned into a 'mumsy bore'. Was everything she spoke about centred around Kitty? Why had she never noticed until now? She was paranoid about her insensitivity to Clara, who was masking her maternal urges by partying harder than the rest of them.

The 4x4 fell silent again.

* * * * *

Edna had an errand at a studio in Camden before heading to Dande's. She was running late and had to jump in a cab. The kids were back at school and the traffic was at a standstill. In the end she had to abort mission and catch the train to Queen's Park. As she pondered how to break the news to Dande...in her own house...one-time model booker Edna spotted a strikingly beautiful boy in his mid-teens with blonde Afro hair and green eyes. Unable to resist talent-spotting, Edna tried to catch the eye of the gangly hoody-wearing lad, but he kept his head down as the train pulled away.

* * * * *

Dande sat cross-legged in her Moorish conservatory, facing her Buddha statue, burning lavender incense and a tea light. She closed her eyes and began to meditate in an attempt to lower her anxiety levels. She thought that the horrendous, Ibiza 'come-down' would have subsided by now. That made her even more anxious. Her sleeping was sporadic. She resisted the temptation to take Tramadol. Her six-year-old, Lola was the only sweet and stable thing in her life. She wanted to be a better mum to her than her own mum was.

Dande Lyon had calmed down as she got older, but the underlying thread of angst was ever present. Bertie was a pain and Eli needed to commit to her once and for all. These thoughts swimming around her mind, had to be suspended for a moment. Dande, was on the precipice of dreams her stage school experience had inspired. She was forced to attend because she was a "handful". She was a 'hot-head' then and the same could still be said of her now. Recognising her weakness was the first step, she told herself. She could do this. Just calm the fuck down and lighten up.

The door-knocker broke her trance. She ran to greet her friends.

"Heeeeyyyy! Come in, come in, guys…"

"We come bearing a bit a Bolly," enthused Clara.

"Nice one…thank-you. I've got cocktails on the go, or should we wait for the others?"

"Break out the shots. Wa-hey. Got any Sambuca?"

"Silly question, Clara, dearest. Haha…"

Just as she ran to her drinks globe, the door went again.

"Piper. Mwaw, mwaw…come in, hun. Oh Edna… mwah, mwah. Did you come together?"

"Oh no, nooo! I literally just arrived at the same time. Sorry I'm late."

"Oh, don't worry. Come in. Grab a seat in the lounge."

"Are they here? Is that Piper?" yelled Clara.

"Bring the drinks through to the lounge, guys…"

ordered Dande. "Just setting up here."

"I do love your place, Dande. When I buy, you've got to help me decorate," complimented Edna.

"Aww, that means a lot, I'd love to. Would you like a cocktail?"

"Yes, I'll have whatever everybody else is having, please."

Dande had spent hours over a vegetable tagine, which she was serving with rose water-infused flat breads. Edna had not expected that and realised she had to hold onto her news a while longer.

She had garnered far more about the ladies than before and was mildly surprised at their dynamics.

She spent time explaining the sad truth about the media and how many unforeseen things could alter the outcome of a programme at any time. The examples she gave had them gripped. She explained how household names didn't always get a green light and how it was hard for them to come to terms with major decisions. Who held the power and how luck played its part. Just when a celebrity thought there time was up, the great comeback magic wand would suddenly strike.

The ladies held onto her every noun and pronoun.

"Yes, so anyway, my point is…it goes to show that in this business expect the unexpected," surmised Edna.

"And erm…so Edna…did you say you've had some info on our show?" interjected Piper.

"Hahaha…er…yes. Yes, guys."

Edna shuffled about on the velvet sofa, avoiding eye contact, rolling her ankles, admiring her ankle boots.

"Okay. I have to be straight with you. There were mixed bag reviews of the edited pilot…and we didn't have a unanimous agreement about the direction we wanted to take the show."

"Did it get commissioned?" persisted Clara.

"Well, yes, but there is one major setback, and I'm so sorry to tell you..."

"Tell us what?" demanded Dande.

"Let her finish..." urged Piper.

"No, it's okay. So, the casting team and our exec...they've given it the go ahead...but...I'm sorry to say, Dande, it will be without you."

Dande slumped back in her seat and stared squarely at Edna, willing her to admit she was mistaken.

Everyone else was in shock.

"How come?"

"No way!"

"Are you joking?"

"What the...."

They were all screeching in horror. Turning to each other, and affectionately hugging Dande...trying to console her.

Dande sat their motionless. Numbed, expression-less, hurting.

"Edna. Please explain," demanded Nancy.

"I don't wanna hear it actually..." said Dande, her lower lip beginning to tremble.

"Oh D...what do you want us to do?" asked Suki.

"We won't do anything without your say. All for one, hey?" Nancy rubbed her on the back.

"No, no. This is a great opportunity so don't let me stop you!" pleaded Dande.

"Fucking hell, Edna. You could've warned us about this!" Piper scolded in support.

Dande nodded gratefully that for the first time in weeks her bestie showed some loyalty.

"Please guys. I'm really ever so sorry to be the

bearer of such bad news. But the series has been commissioned for one season only. Bear with me. They're not going to air the pilot. It wasn't up to me. I fought your corner, Dande, believe me. But Gillian our exec and the channel bosses don't always see the human side. It's all about business and commercialism. Nothing personal. So sorry my love."

Edna took a deep breath.

"Are we expected to carry on without our girl, then?" quizzed Clara.

"Well, it is up to you. We will want to know by end of play tomorrow at the latest. They're prepared to audition new faces - yes, I know it looks mercenary. But this the business of show. It's a heartbreaking game. I never wished you into this position."

"Just like that? Next!" exclaimed Piper.

Edna pursed her lips and nodded reluctantly.

"Look, I had better go. Like I said, let me know what you decide. It'll be a shame if you can't continue."

Edna stood up and tried to kiss Dande goodbye.

"So sorry Dande. Things can and often do change."

She paused looking at a family photo on the wall, "Is that your boy? He has a unique look, think I saw him in Camden earlier. Anyway, I'll personally see if I can find a way round this. I'll be in touch."

Dande winced. What was she talking about?

Edna solemnly kissed the ladies before seeing herself out.

"Has she gone?"

Dande put on a brave face, but she couldn't believe this disastrous turn of events took place in her own home. She wanted to be alone, but that was going to be impossible.

As soon as the door closed the ladies rallied round. There was nothing they could say to console, a now tearful Dande.

"Stop fussing guys, no-one has died. It's just a TV programme…"

"Exactly my thoughts, hun," said Suki.

"If you want my opinion, I meant what I said. You should still do it. Don't worry about me. I don't want to stand in your way."

Dande made a wobbly, noble speech.

"Hey, let's not talk about this now." Clara was wiping away Dande's tears and fixing her hair.

"But you've only got until tomorrow? I swear guys, you will regret it if you don't and resent me as well. I will feel guilty if you don't. So see sense. I'll get over it."

"I can't do it without you. It won't feel right. I'm happy to step down."

Nancy was adamant.

"Please, darling," Dande took Nancy's hand. "Please hear me. I will feel even more shit about it if you don't. Don't make this harder for me. I'm gutted. I should've watched my temper. Edna's right. I wasn't professional. And that's that."

"Alright. Alright, my darling. Listen, listen…"

Nancy held Dande's chin.

"If we do this show, we will do it for you and by God, we will pester them until we get you back on. At least once we're in, and they have got to know us better, we can do some persuading…when we have more clout."

"Nancy's right," agreed Piper. "Once we've got a foothold in with them, we can call a few shots. Right now, we're replaceable. Tch!"

"You mean, make the change from within?"

added Suki.

"Well, it's all we've got. But whatever happens, my darling buddy, we have got your back. Okay?"

Nancy leaned in and smothered her in baby kisses until the rest joined in.

Cracking a smile, Dande pushed them off her, "Get off me, you ratbags, hahaha…Fuck 'em. I need a line? We all in?"

Clara waved a Chinese embroidered pouch in the air…

"Emergency nose-up mini pack at the ready! Let's tuck in."

Clara swiftly set about carefully making space on the side table with the ornate silver tea platter and racked up some fat lines, giving Dande the honour of first go.

They refilled their glasses and barely 15 minutes passed before they snorted a second line.

"I fancy some red? Anyone else?" Dande offered… and the sesh was on. Her pals couldn't leave her. Clara was dishing out the gear, which made it harder still to steer themselves away. Nancy and Piper made calls to organise extended childcare with their hubby and mother respectively. Dande's little girl Lola was already staying with Nanna Lyon, who would take her to school in the morning.

By 3.45am in the early hours everyone had clambered off her sofas. Overall, it was a fun, messy evening, despite the underlying disappointment for the Five-Go-Hard.

Dande climbed the stairs heavily, calling after Bertie just in case he had snuck back in. But he wasn't there. She would have to confess to Eli that this was not the first time Bertie had stayed out overnight. She cried herself to sleep.

The Show Must Crack On

First thing Friday morning Edna emailed Dande with a grovelling apology. In it she assured her that a headed paper hard copy was to follow with confirmation from the lawyers that the pilot will never be broadcast. It was the final nail…

For the rest of the Five-Go-Hard it was a flood of group emails from the production company. They hadn't even agreed to take the offer yet.

Edna called Piper and asked her to set up another WhatsApp group…entitled The Housewives of House…but they needed to talk first.

"Hi Piper, you free to chat?"

Something illegible mumbled back at her.

"Jesus wept? Is that you?"

"Yep…had a late night, keeping Dande company?"

"Hope she was alright after I left?"

"Let's say she's had better nights…anyway, what's up?"

"Well, the big question…did you guys decide to be in the show without Dande?"

"We've not talked about it properly yet, we did have a late one."

"Just vying for a heads-up on the situation. What your impression?"

"Yeah," groaned Piper. "I think the feeling is that we'll do it. But until I check in today, things could've changed...so actually, I don't know now?"

"Fine, sorry Piper. Perhaps keep this under your hat, but you are the one we want as the focal point. The show will centre around you. That is if you still fancy it. So, I'll leave it with you to get the others onside."

"Oh? Oh? Tha'...thank you. Thank you, I don't know what to say?" said Piper, genuinely stunned.

"Well, think about things. This is a fantastic opportunity and hope to hear from you all informally. Preferably before 4 o'clock today. Well done, though, darling. Speak later!"

Piper got out of bed to her dressing area, still in her black camisole top and knickers from the night before, and just stared at herself. A reality show centred around her? This person looking back from the full-length mirror. Was that phone call for real or were the drugs messing with her head? Time was she would have bitten Edna's hand off for this chance. She had befriended her because of her glamorous connections, after all. But now, all she wanted to do was spend her time snatching private moments with Eli. An already complicated situation made worse with cameras about she considered.

She convinced herself Dande would have left Eli for a TV show in a heartbeat, given half a chance. Then he would have been all hers. Her drug-addled mind meandered down a dead-end lane of speculation.

By lunchtime, the Five-Go-Hard WhatsApp group trickled with the odd commiseration for Dande. The newly set up Housewives of House group was a buzzing hive of activity by contrast.

Dande was on the way to collect Lola from her school. Bertie had stayed out all night, but had taken himself to school from wherever he had been. While she waited in the Range Rover she sent yet another message to Eli, who was at his weekend residency in Ibiza. Every week he came home on a Monday and was back out by Wednesday/Thursday...throughout the season. He hadn't come up for air. Poor signals and bad wifi added to her frustration. Dande was feeling desperately lonely, but was trying to hold it together for Lola.

Piper was also on the school run and about to confirm that she, Nancy, Clara and Suki would sign up to the first ever series of The Housewives of House. She was nervous about making the call, but was intercepted by Edna anyway.

"Hi, Piper, have you made a full recovery?"

"Not really, actually. Just picking up the kids from school."

"Did you get a chance to talk to the girls? Sorry to push, I'm just desperate to stop my boss from re-casting."

"Well, this was a really hard decision for us all, as we've been friends with Dande for a long time, but we have agreed to do it. The answer is 'yes'. We're just trying to take it all in."

"Yesss. Phew. I was worried. I promise you won't regret it. We'll make sure you have the most fun! Bear with me, while I notify the production team. Don't be alarmed by the pile of emails and meetings to follow."

"Shit, are we expected to sign our lives away for this?"

"It will feel a bit like that, but promise you, it's just telly stuff...arrrgh! So excited for you all. Congratulations, you're gonna be a reality star!"

"Don't, you're scaring me now."

"Well, don't be. Tell the others, we'll be in touch. Have a fantastic weekend."

Piper hung up, pulled over and texted the girls:

We are in guys. We're the The Housewives of House! Someone better let Dande know please.

Then she double-parked her 'Chelsea tractor' and walked over to the school gates with a new-found air of confidence she almost didn't recognise in herself. As she air-kissed some of the other mothers and friends waiting, an inner voice came from nowhere.

"I'm going to be a "Housewife of…."

As she looked around at some of the other mums in the playground, she muttered: "Soon you lot will probably want to either crawl up my arse…or shun me…hahaha!"

Sharing Is Caring

Dande spent more time at the Al Anon and AA meetings. Bored, with her friends now on the missing list.

The comfort of the new Nike Cortez trainers in the pink and grey colour way, flattered Dande's Amazonian frame. She couldn't help admiring her latest online purchase. She hung out with some of the other mums at school, using playdates as a way of networking. But they were a little too 'straight' for her, as they did not get 'involved'. Partying on a school night practically unheard of.

While she fiddled with the laces of her new kicks, Christopher, the silver fox CEO tapped her on the shoulder and asked her why she had been attending more than usual. Their conversation went beyond niceties and they decided to continue at one of the smarter coffee shops in Notting Hill.

"So he keeps on disappearing? How old is he?"

Christopher was a good listener.

"Bert? He's nearly 14. Way too young, I know he's tall, but I still worry."

"What does Eli think?"

"He does it when Eli goes out of the country. So… Eli doesn't know about the overnights. I never tell him. All I say is that he's bunking off school and that he slams the door. Is that bad?"

"I would say, that you're doing the best you can,

117

but you really should tell Eli. What're you afraid of?"

"Darling, I shouldn't be offloading to you like this, but you're a good listener."

"I'm interested. We're not at the AA because we've got all the answers. Tell me why you're not telling him."

"Because, he'll think I can't manage - which I can't. I think…I think Eli will blame me and leave me."

"He loves you. I'm sure you've got that wrong."

"He thanks me every day for taking on his son, so I get that it means everything to him, but it is me who has to look after him. He's away so much and I'm the one single parenting, hands on…24/7."

"Dande, that's no way to live. There's clearly a lot going on there. Only wish I could help. So you say Bertie has been spotted in Camden?"

Dande looked over her cup at Christopher, batting his pale grey/blue saucer eyes.

"Well, I'm not sure I've got it from a reliable source, but yeah."

"You also say his gran lives in Primrose Hill? Could he have gone there?"

"Oh? I suppose he could, but they're not particularly close. She was the actress, Claudia Flint-Dunn. Selfish cow."

"Really? And her daughter is his mum. The one you talk about at the meetings?"

"Yes. Look, I've never given their identity away before. You won't tell anyone will you?"

"No, promise,"

Christopher reached out his hand, resting it on hers.

"You can tell me anything. I like that you trust me."

"Thank you. I haven't had a chance to really confide in anyone in a while. The story is so stale among my friends."

"Yes, you were saying…"

"Well, you may have heard of Amy Dunn? The tabloid wild child?"

"No way, she's Claudia Flint-Dunn's daughter?"

"Yes, she is also Eli's ex and Bertram's mother."

Christopher, on the face of it a provincial character who lived between London and Cheshire, wore smart suit shirts in pink or stripes, chinos when he wasn't in suit pants. He was always clean-shaven and impeccably groomed. Still married, he claimed he was separated from his wife while she sought treatment for her drinking problems.

Like, Dande, he had joined Al-Anon for advice to help his family, only to discover he had drinking problems of his own stemming from control issues. He, like Dande, was deemed a functioning alcoholic.

The new friends continued to bond over a couple of hours drinking herbal teas, before Dande had to collect Lola. She did not read that Christopher's interest in her was more than platonic. From here on they would meet up before and after meetings connecting as friends. With no alcohol involved she fooled herself that this was a harmless relationship. She valued having someone care about her life's ups and downs when it seemed no one else cared.

Dande's striking beauty beguiled Christopher. He had never met anyone quite like her before. The more he got to know about her, the more he convinced himself that he was in love with her. Everything about his life had been carefully considered. She drew him into a world that was anything but, which stoked his fantasy. He had the key to her happiness. He could rescue her and be her hero, if she would allow him. All he had to do was bide his time. He was not a man of rash decisions.

Sign Off

Once the series had been agreed, and the formal paperwork put to bed, there was a matter of assigning production team roles and getting contracts signed from HR.

Emilee was really concerned about whether she was going to be promoted. She had been called in for a chat with Edna and separately with Charlotte.

Both wanted to sound her out. She wasn't the only intern they had. What were her ambitions, her outlook on popular culture, for instance? Was she left leaning or apolitical. How did she use social media for personal use? Edna was seeking out her creative skills, whereas Charlotte was looking for character. Did she have the stomach for the less savoury parts of the job. Being yelled at, the long hours and the seemingly thankless hard work.

Both had stern advice for her. Edna warned her: "Commitment to one side of the camera is essential. Take your pick and stick to it."

Ann in HR had called her in finally and she sat in the office to face her fate. She was sure that her stint as an intern would not be extended. But she needn't have worried, as her worst fears were allayed, being appointed with her first full-time TV contract.

"Mum! Guess what?"

"Ems, is that you? Guess what? I can't guess. Just tell me…"

"I've only got my first contract. I've got a job on the series. An actual job."

"How much they paying you?"

"It's not about the money yet. I needed to get started. Can't believe it."

"That's lovely news. Your Dad will be happy. Do you want me to tell him?"

"No, I'll do it. When's he back?"

"About 8ish, I think."

"Perfect. I'll probably be pissed by then, though... hahaha..."

"Ems, watch yourself. You'll get fired before you've even started."

"Never. I told you, they're all pissheads here. I'm amazed they get anything done."

"Sounds to me like you're the one doing everything actually..."

"Oh, Mummy!"

*****

Between October and November, building up to filming at the start of 2017, there were meetings after meetings...on top of more meetings...with lawyers, agents and various members of the production team.

The impact on the Five-Go-Hard group's social activity was devastating for Dande. The Housewives of House were so busy they simply could not make time (or find the energy) to get together with Dande anymore. She stopped inviting them over for sushi, because their excuses were always Housewives of House related. Her friends had become as time poor as their DJ husbands.

The Ibiza closing season long gone, for the guys it

was back to UK club night residencies for a while, except for the odd jaunt to Dubai, Berlin or Istanbul. The DJs arranged to meet for a late afternoon pow-wow, a 'boys one' down the pub over a few beers. Eli was included.

"Anyone else getting a burger?" enquired late arrival Eli.

"Yes, we've got some coming. Pay at the bar."

"Shit, forgot, Dande's cooking for me...but I'll get one anyway...it'll probably be one of her awful tagines for me later."

Now seated, the lads didn't waste time getting stuck into the conversation.

"Good idea this, Charlie," said Eli. "Been meaning to have a chat about this reality show business."

"Yeah, what's everyone's take on it?" quizzed Flemming.

"Well, first of all, Eli. You want to thank your lucky stars Dande's not in it," claimed Charlie. "The amount of time Piper is either on the phone, or running off here...or there. At all kinds of times. It's been Housewives this, Housewives that! It's beginning to affect the kids."

"Ah, you as well? It's all getting on my fucking nerves. Clara is a handful at the best of times, but she's changing. We're meant to be trying for a baby. Now she says she wants to see if they'd make a 'storyline' out of it. I mean...a fucking storyline? It's our lives, not a TV show."

"Mate, sorry to hear that," said Charlie, patting Flemming on the back. "It's gonna happen for you soon, mate. You'll see."

"I know what he means. Nancy's been the same," chipped in Baxta. "She's been taking Poppy with her everywhere. I don't think she should be in that environment. Every time I say anything I get it in the neck."

"Like what?"

"Like, "oh you're always swanning off, playing out. You don't have to do anything at home. It's her time to think about herself for a change, you know, that kinda shit."

"What's Suki been like Razr?"

"Hmmm? Suks has been a mare as well. She's never home. Between the show stuff she's either going back with Nancy or Clara or something. It's like she doesn't want to come home anymore?"

Razr downed the rest of his pint. "Menopause Behaving Badly," he added wryly.

"I don't see it like that," said Eli. "I think it's worse for me with Dande left out. She is ex-drama school. She's been so depressed. Without the distraction, she's on me all the time. All needy and shit! And the girls seem to have abandoned her because of the very show she was desperate to be in!" Eli's added emphatically.

"She's not back on the sauce, is she?" said Flemming concerned. "Clara's borderline alcoholic herself."

"No, she's been going to more meetings than she used to weirdly."

"Seriously, what can we do about it?" pondered Baxta out loud.

The posh burgers started arriving on slate platters and Eli got up to get a round in. Baxta's was a pertinent question. The time for complaining had past. The threat to their lifestyle and relationships hung in the balance. Their wives had signed away their privacy. Damage limitation wasn't even an option. The TV production company inadvertently owned them too.

What's It All About Bertie?

Armed with a new approach to the Bertie problem after her chats with Christopher, Dande was cooking up a storm. She hoped Eli would have come home before Lola went to bed at 8.30pm, but he was late for the family dinner. She had made his favourite Moroccan chicken tagine in the clay pot.

"Eli? Is that you?"

"Sorry I'm late, hun. Just gonna freshen up…"

Out of a force of habit, post post-coital sessions with Piper, Eli ran up the stairs to their bathroom ensuite, avoiding eye contact with Dande, careful to scrub off the day's residue.

Dande was extremely suspicious of this altered behaviour because she was always scolding him for not washing his grubby hands after being in the studio.

Insisting she didn't want to hear any excuses, she shoved the chicken dish at him and moaned how it had dried out.

Picking at her own plate, Dande approached Eli like she spoke to Christopher. For some reason she was calmer around him.

"Eli…I've been thinking about what we could do to help Bertie get back on track."

"Yeah? And what's that?"

"Don't shout at me, but every time you've had a gig abroad or doing the graveyard shift at the studio…"

"Yes?"

"Well, Bertie hasn't just been bunking off school. He's been running away and disappearing overnight. When he comes back…I mean, he always comes back…but he never tells me where he's been. At first I thought it was a phase. But it's been happening more and more and it's got out of hand!"

"You what? Why didn't you tell me?!"

Eli spat out chicken bits.

"I said, don't shout!"

"What if he's been gang banging or something?"

"Shssh. He's upstairs. He'll hear you."

"I don't fucking care, D. This is not on!"

"I knew you'd react like this. Just stop a minute. I was talking to someone at Al Anon and they got me thinking. What if he's been going to Granny Claudia's?"

"Hanagabout… Claudia's in Primrose Hill? How's he getting up there? Didn't think that they were particularly close."

"He's almost 14. He can go anywhere he pleases and he flaming well does, by all accounts."

"What's been going on here? Has she said anything?"

"Well, no. But, he was seen in Camden. Actually, I'm not sure if it was him."

"Do you know something, Dande? You are not making any sense."

Eli stood up from the table and stomped towards the hallway stairs, and bellowed:

"Bertie!"

"Don't!"

"Why not?"

"I have a plan. Rather than come down heavy on him. Why don't you pretend you're going away on a gig. We follow him and see where he goes. Then depending on where it is we approach him about it."

"What spy on him? Stupid, stupid idea. He'll never trust us after that."

"He doesn't trust us now! At least this way we have a chance of getting some truthful answers."

"I don't like it. I hate the lying and deceiving."

"Hmmm. That's rich coming from you…"

"Sorry?"

"Forget it. Let's focus on Bertie. I am so worried about him. We're not sharing parental responsibilities fairly. I get the brunt of it. I'm losing the will. I am, I swear, Elijah!"

Eli conceded and calmed down. He knew he had dropped the ball here. The boy needed his dad around more.

That night in bed, Eli was under the covers with Dande nestled in the exact space Piper liked to be. He cradled his missus.

"Dande."

"Hmm?"

"I know I've always said it, but I mean it. I appreciate all you do for this family. Bertram has always been a handful, not just nowadays. You have always been patient with him as well. More than I would. It warms my heart when I think how much we both love him. Our little Lola Lyon is the icing on the cake. She's just so cute, I know she's mine, but she is."

"Hmmm, what's got into you?"

"Wait. What I'm trying to say is…is…will you marry me?"

Dande sprang upright like the Bride of Frankenstein defibrillated. It was dark, but the lights from the street were just enough to see his face.

"Are you? Eli? Yes! Yes! Yes!" she screamed, kissing and hugging him with a breathless intensity he had never felt from her before.

"That's a yes then, I take it?" joked Eli.

"Elijah Stefano, don't be fucking with me. It's not funny. You better mean it this time?"

"Come here you turkey! I have never been more serious. I love you, no matter what, I always have."

He pulled her to him and planted an intimate kiss on her mouth.

"Have you got a ring?"

"Er, nope, not yet…"

"Let's get one tomorrow. I'm not taking any chances. I want that ring!"

"I mean it. I'm serious. Love you my beautiful, Dande Lyon."

"Babe, I don't know if I can sleep. I wanna tell my mum and the girls…You've made me so happy. I don't think you know."

"I think I do. Congratulations, we're engaged, now go to sleep."

"After everything that's happened lately, you've made everything worthwhile. It pisses on that stupid show anyway!"

"Fuck them Dande. Arse 'oles!"

Positions Please

Pre-production meetings continued one into another. Schedule after updated schedule, call sheet after call sheet, with location decisions, for each of The Housewives of House. Shooting at their homes, spas, beauty parlours….and at bars, nightclubs and pubs…also hotels and parks. As key members of the west London's boho set, there was no shortage of thriving places to shoot. Queens Park, Kensal Rise, Westbourne Grove, Portobello, Notting Hill, South Kensington, West Hampstead, Kings Road and Knightsbridge all places of interest in London Town.

The camera's floodlight had a way of glamming up even the blandest of locations on the dullest days. The Housewives of House basked under the spotlight they received while filming, while the general public pointed fingers and got their smart phones out. It fed into their previously suppressed grandiose sense of self, which was not just a mother, a wife, a daughter, but someone in their own right, that mattered. It was addictive.

At one shoot a message popped up on the old Five-Go-Hard WhatsApp group.

We are officially engaged! Love Dande and Eli xx

They promptly informed the production team explaining their lack of concentration that day because they had become preoccupied with some great news. Together they announced Dande's engagement with zeal. With one exception, Piper who was less than enamoured and schemed to end this preposterous idea once and for all as soon as she could get her hands on Eli. She could see right through this 'act'.

It had to be Dande who had forced poor-put-upon-Eli into it, in desperation for some attention after being axed from the series.

In light of this news, behind closed doors, the production crew were called for one of those extraordinary meetings in confidence to discuss whether they should bring Dande back and persuade her to tie the knot in the series finale.

The Housewives of House would continue, as is, with some build-up stories, such as planning a hen party, or shopping for wedding outfits, culminating in a huge wedding spectacular/bust up.

Was the idea off the mark? Would it make up for dropping Dande from the line up or would she kick off at their audacity? They unanimously agreed to try and get Dande on board. Casting producer Laura Cave and series editor Gillian Morris-Quaid and a few other channel bosses were called in now. They were all in agreement, but they knew, with so much potential tension running through the rest of the series, with Dande's reinstatement it would become an even more delicate operation to pull off.

One that would have to be carefully stage-managed. Maybe they should broach it with ladies of The Housewives of House first. See if any of them objected. Failing that, throw money at it, and pay for the wedding, pay for anything that would make it happen. They wanted this storyline to run, whatever it took. Edna Wright had the closest relationship with 'the talent' out of any of the production crew. They laid the responsibility to pull this off firmly at her door.

Edna's first move saw her take The Housewives of House out for a personal catch up a few days later. She ordered lunch for them at newly-opened restaurant The Ivy, Kensington and carefully ran the idea past them, omitting the part where her reputation at work was at stake.

"So guys, do you think Dande would be up for it? She hasn't set a date yet, has she?"

"Not being funny, Edna," said Nancy, defensively. "Dande was so hurt about everything. I mean, it would be a nice thing for her, but it's not up to us."

"Exactly. I get that. I was hoping we could make it up to her by featuring her wedding in the finale. Bad idea?"

"Yes, bad idea actually!" said Piper defiantly. "I know her well enough to know that her pride took a beating, especially as she's so vulnerable right now... and Eli would never agree to it anyway. Nah," she scoffed.

Piper gestured for the other Housewives of House to agree with her.

"Despite what has happened I have always been in Dande's corner. Could one of you just sound her out anyway? You're her friends. Besides, I'm not sure I'd have much sway."

"Leave it with us then," asserted Suki. "We're probably the ones best positioned to gauge her mood."

The 'Housewives' wondered how they could find the time, in between filming, and their domestic day-to-day schedules – doctor's appointments, weekends away to see in-laws, parents' evenings, birthdays and family functions – just to meet up with Dande. They hadn't done so in a while.

"I think we have to make it our priority. Dande must wonder about us. I certainly miss her," came Suki's rallying cry.

"Me too. I feel guilty sometimes and it kinda spoils it for me. If we could get her on side…" insisted Clara.

'Yeah, it's bittersweet," sighed Nancy.

"Well, let's sort something now. My place, the next free morning?"

Nancy's house was down the road in Queen's Park…same as Dande. They rarely ended up at hers because Dande was ever the hostess.

"She's at AA some mornings so check first…" suggested Clara.

True to form, not everyone was so positive about Dande's possible return.

"I just don't think it's a good idea…not with how she kicked off during the pilot. Short memories," sneered Piper, dismissively.

Nevertheless, Suki took the reins to organise their catch up with Dande. Nato may be obsolete, but she was the diplomatic relations of the group.

*****

"Eli look at this message. The girls have invited me to Nancy's place. But it's like, in the morning…I think something's up. Dunno why…"

"Are you going?"

"I don't want to, but I will…I suppose."

"You can change your mind. Just walk out if they try anything. Make sure they're not filming either."

* * * * *

Knowing Nancy's influence as the voice of reason, Piper made sure she arrived early and got in first.

"I'm worried about us raking everything up again, Nance, with me and Dande...well things aren't the same. We've drifted apart."

"I can tell. We all can. But don't you think by including her in this small way, we can show her how much we still love her? And it would be a chance for you two to really make up."

"I can see that, but what if she turns into Bridezilla? It'll be me that suffers the brunt of it. I don't trust the production crew not to set us up."

"Yes, there is a risk, but she is a diva and we love her for it, right? What I don't get, in fact none of us get, is why she is so down on you in the first place?"

The phone rang.

The others had arrived, gathered outside in the pathway that led up to Nancy's three-bedroomed ground floor garden flat. She beckoned them through the open-plan reception-come-kitchen area.

"Hey! Come in guys...is Dande not with you?"

"Hiya!" screamed Dande, waving her ring finger, running past the brick wall fencing trying to catch up with Clara and Suki. "I'm here!"

The reaction to her engagement ring was the kind that the production company craved. The cacophony of admiration filled the house. Meanwhile, Piper's heart sank to her stomach, twisted in knots.

"It's gorgeous!"

"You lucky thing. Congratulations."

"You deserve it, darling. Mwah!"

"Let me have another look?"

"Where d'ya get it?"

"Yes, tell us everything!"

"Didn't think Eli had it in him!"

"I know, I know. I can't tell you how happy I am."

"Yes, you can. I'll make some bucks fizz…let me grab the champers," cried Nancy, actually starting to blub a little bit.

"Silly. You'll set us all off," sobbed Clara.

Feeling relaxed with all the love in the room, Dande started to tell the story of how Eli randomly proposed in bed.

Immediately, Piper thought the worst and imagined the happy couple making love shortly afterwards. She wasn't sure she could stand to listen to any more. It was absolute torture. Dande had a captive audience. This was her moment and she was going to milk it. She was the only unmarried one in the group. They had The Housewives of House…and this engagement was hers.

"…so I made him take me to Boodles the next day. I cancelled everything! There was no way I was going to let him off. I'd told him to propose with a ring when he was ready. But it's Eli. I thought he'd never get round to it. Should've known that. Anyhoo, he was still up for it. I swear, I pinched myself in the Uber all the way to Sloane Street. I knew which ones I liked…it was a matter of how much he was willing to spend on it…hahaha. So this is the one we agreed on!" concluded Dande her fingers outstretched capturing the clarity of the square stone.

"How much was it? Go on, tell us," goaded Clara, screwing her face up, wiping away a tear.

"I can't tell you that. But, let's just say we're a long way from affording a wedding any time soon. He spent more on it than he planned." said Dande looking down on her bling admiringly.

"So how soon would you marry him if money was no object?" began Nancy, orchestrating the ladies to let her continue the line of questioning.

"Erm…like, yesterday! Lola would be such a cute little flower girl as well. She's just the right age."

"Dande. What if you could have a wedding, late Spring, all expenses paid…would you do it?"

"Er…yeah. Silly question. But that's never gonna happen! Hah!"

"Well, what if I told you that it could…?" said Nancy tentatively.

"What are you getting at Nance? I knew you were all up to something. Is this some kind of set up? Secret filming?" panicked Dande.

"Slow down, hun,"

Nancy was almost ready to abort mission seeing the expression on her face.

"Hear me out a sec. The Housewives of House has come between us all…in one way or another. We thought perhaps there was a way of making it up to you. So, what if The Housewives of House agreed to feature your wedding in the show? There I said it!"

Dande was flabbergasted by the onslaught of suggestions that followed. They pulled her in various directions and counter argued her negativity. Dande would take some convincing. Piper remained subdued.

"Guys, I'm thinking about it, don't get carried away. Hahaha. I thought you'd all gone off me."

"Yay…" came the two-finger applause from Clara.

"Piper, do you think I should do this?"

"It's not up to me, though, is it?"

"It is actually. I always said you'd be my Maid of Honour…"

"Aww…" Suki curled her bottom lip.

Never had anyone had to dig deeper to summon up an acceptable smile in such a conflicting situation. Piper realised she would have to drag the hem of the darkest dress of duplicity around for the foreseeable, if Dande accepted. The only option was to play along until she found a way to prevent the junket from exploding.

"Babe. If it means you'll do it, I will be your Maid of Honour."

And the Oscar goes to Mrs Fenchurch aka Piper Blair.

She couldn't resist adding a passive aggressive dig. "Better run it by Eli first, though…"

The Housewives of House were back, with the original line up and how they let rip at the idea. The impromptu morning gathering had to come to an end as everyone had some other place to be on this one morning off.

Piper assured them she would make the call to Edna as soon as Dande had discussed it with Eli. Before the front door was even open, Dande was on the phone trying to get hold of her fiancé. Piper grabbed her hand forcefully and yelled, "What are you doing?"

A little unnerved at this overreaction, Dande explained, "Calling Eli…why?"

"Erm…"

"He always takes so long to pick up…just thought I'd start trying now."

"Darling, sorry. Doh! It's just that if you really want to persuade Eli to do this wedding, wouldn't it be better talking to him about it in person first - face to face. It's a big ask…" rescued Piper.

"You're right babe…didn't think of that. I'll make his favourite dinner. He's going to be sick of chicken tagine by the time the wedding is over. Imagine me? Married! Arrrgh…"

Dande promptly kissed Piper on both cheeks in gratitude.

*****

As soon as she was in the car, Piper called Eli, who picked up first time. "What's up Piper! Told you to text first."

"It's urgent."

"Not about the engagement? Seriously?"

"Well, yes. Get used to it. Dande is going to ask you if you can get married on the show."

"What! The Housewives of House? Does she even want to?"

"No, but the girls talked her round. It was the producer's idea. I think you need to call it off."

"Call off the engagement? We haven't even set a date for the wedding yet. You're not telling me what to do, Piper."

"I'm just saying if you don't get a grip of this situation there's going to be trouble. Not from me. These telly people are rottweilers. Talk her out of it. For your own sake."

"Fuck off Piper. I decide what I'm doing. Please text me first next time. Don't call again."

"Hang on a minute. Remember she doesn't know you know. So act dumb. Stupid. And you, go fuck yourself."

Reset

The production team sent a car to pick up Dande and Eli for a snazzy lunch at Quagalino's with the channel bosses and Gillian Morris-Quaid, Laura Cave and Edna Wright.

The happy-couple-to-be knew they were being schmoozed and took to it well, guzzling down the bottles of expensive wine at the fine dining table. The posh accents and suits spoiled what was an otherwise memorable lunch. Eli and Dande had already agreed between themselves to accept the offer. However, they wanted to let them sweat while they sussed out their options.

This DJ and his own Housewife of House appeared bolshie about the opportunity presented to them, but they underestimated the TV people. They held all the cards, the key to unlocking money in them there telly hills and had left many wannabees behind still panning for fame gold, while the stakes were too high. A big yawn for them to sit though, and play the game, but a necessary by product of their world. Edna was beyond relieved at how the plans were transpiring.

Over the coming weeks it was just the planning stages for Dande, no filming. Her shoot times were for the big reveal, taking place on the big day. However, the meetings re: cake, dresses, shoes and everything the event planners could bring to the wedding circus took over. She had a head for design and didn't want it to be tacky but trusted them enough to steer her in the right direction. There were a lot of people coming from the music fraternity. Everything had to be on the right side of cool and tastefully stylish. There was one caveat, Reena Qureshi was to steer clear. With so much to agree to, it kept Dande distracted from what the others were up to.

*****

The production meeting room was an uninspired space in the centre of the shared office building. It had a large table with two conference telephone units in the middle and several stylish ergonomic chairs. One clock and multiple power points, the room catered for up to sixteen people. It was going to be a full house with the wedding event planners in attendance, the production team and The Housewives of House. Ironically, Dande was not invited to the preliminary ideas session about her own wedding.

"Looks like we're all here?"

Charlotte raised an eyebrow confirmation with Emilee.

"Before we begin, let's welcome James and Julian Moran from Cater Moran Events with us this morning. Lovely to have you and your staff with us, guys. As you all know, we have decided to run the series finale with Dande's wedding. With our gorgeous Piper in the Maid of Honour storyline. Today is just a briefing for us all to get behind what we are hoping to achieve in the lead up and on the big day. Dorrit will follow up with which unit will be producing this segment. For now, like I said, his is just a brainstorm of ideas to get a clearer picture of how we all see this going. Housewives of House, we need you to tell us how you see the wedding, as you're the ones closet to the happy couple and we're gonna need you to... shall we say...usher them into agreeing with some of our non-negotiables...hahaha. By now, I think you know how we're building for the show."

Charlotte gave one of her most patronising don't-answer-back grimaces to The Housewives of House.

"Before I hand over to Cater Moran, let me remind you that everything being discussed here is under the strictest confidence."

James and Julian went from nautical catering to nuptial events, after planning their own gay wedding, which had been a huge success. They dressed smartly and sharply. They had the same suits made in different colours and patterns and swapped jackets. This became their trademark image. They had worked on a few reality shows before and absolutely ate up the highly-strung turbulence that came with the territory.

Piper fidgeted and fumbled. Every bit of her was aggrieved that she had to sit through more hours of this incessant talk about this wedding. She was allowing her heart to be flagellated by taking part. She had a hand in it. Edna Wright was a casual acquaintance who got out of hand. Like her 'friend-ship' with Eli. She tried to block out the chirpy nature of the 'happy couple' references. If they only knew. She dared herself to stand up and shout: "I'm fucking Eli, you morons! He loves me NOT Dande!"

Dream wedding suggestions abounded across the table with Caribbean beach, yachts on the Med and Scottish castle scenarios. The gushing from the other Housewives of House made her gag...

"Oh I love that one…"

"Wish we had done that for our wedding"

"This one is really romantic."

All Piper had left to give was a generic response.

"Hmmm, I know what you mean."

Followed by fake frantic nods in agreement.

One hour in and she was suffocating. A picture of Dande and Eli taken together in Ibiza was passed around the meeting room table. A slap in the face. Piper jumped up, grabbed her phone and bag and darted out of the meeting…

"Sorry, I've got to take this call."

There was no call, except for the one she was making to Eli as she ran down the stairs.

*****

The sunrays from the atrium skylight beamed straight over Piper as she leaned against the wall, back turned away from what was a secluded area of the TV production studio in West Kensington. It was hard to tell her nails were the reddest of red shellac, with her fingers so tightly gripped to her iPhone.

"Please, please don't tell me you're going to go through with it? Please. I'll leave Charlie, just say…"

Her petite frame in a black leather mini wriggled in discomfort at the response she was receiving on the other end of the phone. For one momentary sob, she caught herself, remembered where she was, and brushed away her tears.

"You've got to stop this from happening. I thought you and me were…"

Piper tailed off her pleas, stammering, unable to scramble any more than she had already made five minutes before. She slumped hopelessly against the corridor wall giving in to the misery and dejection.

"But I'm expected to go back into the meeting. They're all banging on about it and I can't bear it!"

From the top of the mezzanine, Emilee slowed her gait, A4 call sheets in hand, recently promoted from intern to research assistant, trying to locate Piper and bring her back to the production office.

She thought she had the measure of the phone conversation she had overheard. It was crucial enough to see her fast-tracked to the next level of her career...if she was to handle it wisely.

She could hardly believe her yellow-Nike-dunks and black-jeaned luck. Her mentor was right. Being in the right place, right time could make as much of a career impact as good old-fashioned hard work in the industry. Who to tell first, if at all. Series producer Edna Wright or the scarier option, series editor, Gillian Morris-Quaid. She wondered what the payoff would be in the end? Would she get the credit or could such information lead to a bigger contract and pay check? What she didn't want was the proverbial pat on her red curly head. This news was a break-through that could spin the current storyline on its head.

"Piper, you down there?" Emilee sang out with a hop skip and jump towards the stairway.

"Sorry, I've got to shoot off...erm, tell the team I'll be back later."

Emilee sprinted down the stairs to try and catch her, but it was too late, she was already behind the wheel of her Porsche Cayenne, whizzing out of the car park.

The words "never lose sight of the talent" rang through Emilee's ears, as Piper slipped through her fingers.

"Dalmatians…" muttered Emilee, dejectedly.

The leather on leather seat discomfort made a racket as Piper tried to seat belt-up as she took off down North End Road headed towards the Talgath Flyover. She immediately tapped up Dande.

*****

In a Portobello Road church, the tall and intimidating Amazonian Dande, in a grey and lemon cashmere top, peered over the table of thermal tea and coffee pots, fussing about using brown sugar instead of the white refined kind.

"Inspiring today wasn't it? The milk is just there."

"Yes, wasn't it? How are you getting on Dande, you're looking so well as usual."

"Think so? I'm really good, thanks, Christopher. Well, I'm not meant to say, but I might be getting married soon. And it may be filmed for a reality TV show. Anyway…haha, I've said too much already…but I'm dead excited about it. Can't even contain myself. Things are going my way for once."

Silver fox CEO, Christopher, tilted his head with approval, hiding his disappointment at her news. He had held a pipe dream that she would leave her philandering DJ partner, stay clean and live with him instead. There was the small matter of leaving his own wife, of course.

Dande gave him her signature cheeky wink, as she rolled her long raven hair into a loose side bun away from the biscuits. How Christopher lived for that little gesture every week, building on his fantasy of them at the weekly meetings.

If Dande even knew she had this effect on him or any man in her wake, she would have been unbear-

142

able. She already oozed a formidable air of confidence, was brash, loud and in your face. A proper cockney with her French Caribbean heritage, she had never focused on her model looks, but was all too aware that she was misunderstood, regularly rubbing people up the wrong way. She was given to periods of self-reflection and was often disenfranchised as a result.

*****

"Dande, it's me. Where are you?"

"You alright, Piper, lovely?"

"Yes, just nasally…I've just left the production office."

"Fancy a coffee, D?"

"Babe, sorry I can't…you know I'm at the AA Tuesday mornings, I'm on tea urn duty as well, so… is everything alright?"

"Yes, hun, no worries love. Catch you later then."

"No worries, honey! Ciao babe!"

This was exactly what Piper had hoped to hear as she took command behind the wheel of her meteor gray metallic, 4 x 4, and swung a heavy filter at the next turning and headed out of town to Chertsey.

Just A Pipe Dream

Piper tapped her phone, calling via WhatsApp this time, and whispered…

"I'm in the car park. You recording?"

"What, you're outside the studio?"

"I told you, I need to see you. Now."

"You fucking nutter. Wait there. I'm coming out!"

Piper hung up and wiped her sweaty palms against her Sylvia Rykiel knit, her eyes swollen with tears as she stared at the love of her life pushing through the fire doors to meet her.

He opened the passenger door and jumped in, turning to face his teary blue-eyed lover. Eli's heart sank when he saw the state she was in, but composed himself well.

"Piper…Fuck sake. Told you not to call me…or come here."

Eli was totally annoyed and astonished.

"How did you know I was here?"

"You tweeted it, doughnut!"

"Well, Jake's gonna be here in a second so I can only talk for five minutes."

"No he's not! Why're you lying to me?"

"I'm telling you, he's on his way."

"And I'm telling you, he has been tagged on Facebook, in Lisbon?"

"You fucking stalker…seriously…where does Charlie think you are?"

"Thinks I'm filming or something…like he cares…"

"Alright, alright...let's talk inside, but we are going to talk...and you are not gonna like it."

Eli's biceps were bulging out from his stone colour, light-knit, three button Cos shirt as he showed Piper into the stuffy studio. He apologised for not having any refreshments to offer her. She strutted to the four-foot bass speakers and circled the drinks stains with her finger.

"No drinks? Is it any wonder? Have you been mixing tequilas or tunes in here?"

"These are so big. Whack up the music, let me see how loud they can go."

Piper recoiled.

"How big are these speakers? Turn them up, let's see what they've got."

"That, darling, is Big Ben, you've seen it before?"

"Never noticed until now. Go on then...louder!"

"Okay, watch this."

Eli turned away from the leather mini-skirted teaser for just a moment to re-set the track.

Piper was in mischievous mood. The same humour that brought them together would keep them together, she believed.

She was wearing black opaque tights and black ankle boots. She hoisted her upper body diagonally across the speaker. Just holding on with one hand, she swung her right hand behind her and using her nails, pierced a hole through her tights and ripped them open...the struggle alerted Eli from the corner of his eye.

She was commando and baring it all for him, framed by the black nylon, her waxed flesh, powered him up immediately. She peered at him for a brief second or two, her neck distorted. If Eli had any intention of cooling things off, it would have to be after what he was about to do. There was no talk. Only action. The music was the only audible sound. The bass tones ran through the writhing bodies until they couldn't...

The guilt riddled Eli looked on at Piper, as she rolled her ripped tights off and zipped up her ankle boots. The usual banter between them was absent, at odds with the energy of the loud track still blaring.

"I'll just turn this down."

Eli reached for the master volume on the desk.

Piper skimmed through her Mui Mui hand bag for feminine wipes and make up. She was quietly smug at how easy it was to turn him on. Convinced herself that she was irresistible to him.

"Piper. We have to talk."

Eli's voice came from his lower register and serious to the point that Piper was jolted by it.

"Actually, we do. Why do you think I came here?" she countered.

He tried to sense whether that was sarcasm and glared at her.

"You go first, then."

She skulked over to the sofa.

"Have you got a drink?"

"I told you, I haven't got anything in."

"Basically, you know what I have come to say. I want us. I want you to leave Dande. Please, I know she's my friend. But it's also why I know she's not right for you. We get on so well, we laugh at the same things and enjoy the same stuff. I think we balance each other out. It's all got so complicated with The Housewives of House. I can't believe you're actually going to go ahead with a wedding? And have it televised."

"How many times, Piper? I can't let her down. She's the only real mother Bertie knows. For that alone I owe her. Why can't you understand this one point?"

"Because that's not love, that's obligation."

"It is love. She loves me, she loves Bertie and Lola. So, I ..."

"Go on, say it. You love her."

"I said you wouldn't like what I had to say."

"Do you love her?"

"I'm gonna marry her, Pi, I have to."

Piper took a deep breath to heal the wrench in her stomach.

"You can't even say it to me. Do you love her? Eli, do you?"

"It's not a question of love, is it? I love being with you. I love what we've got, but I can't offer you any more than that. What about you and Charlie? He's my mate too..."

"I'm gonna leave him. I'll leave him tonight, just say the word."

"No, no, no, Piper, listen."

Eli walked over to the little beauty, helplessly looking at him before gently whispering to her.

"How did we get this far?"

He scooped her up and held her close to him. She listened to his heartbeat, the warmth of his body, a space she once felt safe in was now bereft and borrowed. It was where Dande probably felt safe too.

"Let's not talk about it anymore, Eli. I'm in too much pain. If you loved me at all you would feel it too?"

"But I do love you, Piper. In any other circumstances, this would be easy. But I have no choice but to go ahead with the wedding. It would break

Dande's heart if I didn't and she would go nuclear on me. She so would."

"No, you don't. You don't love me."

"I do. But it's not just about that is it? Piper, get real! You have Luke and Poppy to think about? How could you do it to them?"

"Don't guilt trip me, mate. Plenty of couples break up. It's never easy. But in the long run, everyone adjusts. They do. What are you scared of?"

"Yeah? I'm fucking shit scared of this actually. It's insane! We'll be hurting too many people. Mrs Lyon would skin me alive. Our mates would be devastated by it. Think of Clara and the girls?"

"After some explaining, they'd be fine."

"You're deluded, darling. Even if we could get together, I couldn't bring Charlie's kids up nor expect you to bring up Bertie and my baby girl! Think about it…"

"Don't you think I've thought about nothing else for the last God knows? Of course I know it would be difficult, but not impossible. I'm a good mother!"

Eli eased away backwards and sat in the swivel chair.

"Piper! This has to stop. We can't do this anymore."

"Don't say it, Eli…don't."

"We can't, fucking get it, will you?"

"No, I can't give you up!"

"We have got the world of cameras on us all. It's too close for comfort."

"Alright…I'll leave the show. How about that?"

"They'd sue the fuck out of you. Get real. You're the one that brought them in…look, I have to get back. I don't think we should talk about this again, at least not until after the wedding."

Those fateful words had Piper in turmoil, power-less to manipulate the situation. She couldn't stand to stand it.

"Babe, this is too much." she said faintly.

"No more, Piper. No more, I'm sorry. Let's talk again when the cameras have gone. I mean it. No calls, no texts, don't come here again either. I'm putting a stop to this before it gets really out of hand. Sorry. It's not forever, okay?"

She nodded forlornly, clinging to the words "it's not forever".

Mol-ing It Over

Ever since overhearing Piper's meltdown on the phone at the production office, Emilee was nesting this little secret egg of reality TV wonder in her mind. What could it all mean in terms of the show? For what reason would Piper not want Dande's wedding to go ahead, she mulled. Piper was to be Maid of Honour, as best friend and star of the show that revolved around her. It was definitely a man she was talking to.

Was there another wedding in their friendship group? Emilee realised she had much to investigate. She went back to Ipswich to her family home for the weekend and confided in her mother about the predicament. They had tea at a local cafe while Emilee took notes from her mother's wise suppositions. She, an avid watcher of soaps, reader of gossip magazines and unravelling of murder mystery dramas.

"When you get back, to speed things up, ask the 'right' questions from the people that know her best."

"It feels like I didn't hear everything properly now, I'm doubting myself."

"Think about everything she said. Say it back to me as if you were her."

"Erm…firstly, don't correct or laugh at me, Mummy. This is just how she speaks."

"Go on then!"

"She said…something…like… 'stop this happening. I love you so much. I'll leave Charlie on your say so'…" mocked Emilee.

"It's definitely another man. This Charlie is her husband then?"

"Yes. She definitely said, 'I'll leave Charlie'. That's why I assumed she must be having an affair."

"Do you think she was talking to one of the other women?"

"No. They were all at the meeting."

"She could have been…"

"No! Wait a sec, Mum…I've got it. She said that we were 'all going on about it'. Yes. That was it. She said…'You have to stop this from happening. They're all going on about it in the meeting'. Whoever it is, must know about the show or be involved."

"So she wants the show to stop, does she?"

"No, she can't do. She has been lapping it up. A diva in the making, that's for sure."

"Let's narrow this down, Ems…What did you talk about in this meeting?"

"It was all about the finale…the final episode of the first series. We had the wedding planner events people in this meeting. Ah! She ran out when they started talking about whether a tux was the right look for a groom, who is a DJ…"

"Who is getting married again?"

"Don't try and trick me Mum, I haven't given you any names."

"You mentioned a Charlie so far…why so secretive. Tch! I won't tell anybody."

"Shssh, Mummmmm, I think I've worked it out. If I'm wrong, I could mess things up big time, but if I am right…fucking hell, I've got goosebumps…oops sorry, swear word!"

"Tch! Please don't go cocking anything up for yourself. Maybe leave well alone this time. You're just starting out," gasped Emilee's mum, a reliable sounding board to her daughter as ever.

*****

The weekend flew by but Emilee was perplexed by the saga. Thinking deeply about Piper's secret conversation again on her train journey back, she wished she could run it by her friends, but that was an absolute no no.

Back at the office, she happened to run in to Edna as they walked into the building together.

"Morning, nice weekend, Em?"

"Good morning, yes, went back home to see the folks."

"Lovely. Where's home?"

"A small village near Ipswich."

"Yes, you may have mentioned that before, sorry. Anyway Emilee, glad I've caught you before they nab you inside. Would you be up for working with me today? I'll square it with the others."

"Erm, sure."

Emilee was both nervous and tickled by this. Perhaps she was finally being groomed for bigger things. With that in mind she wasn't stupid enough to ask what for. This was telly and you did what was asked of you.

"Great, I'll log in and check a few emails before we head off. We'll get a cab. We're meeting the chaps from Cater Moran in town. They're getting us lunch at BAFTA in Piccadilly. Have you been there yet?"

"No. Sounds fantastic."

"Yeah, it's nice there. You can be my second pair of ears."

Emilee reckoned it was fate…She was meant to have this one to one time with Edna who was her mentor, after all. She had also worn her new silver Converse All Stars trainers and BAFTA was the perfect place to christen them.

* * * * *

As they walked up the stairs with the gold BAFTA mask plaques on the wall, Emilee dreamed about receiving one such award (as one or two staff on the production team had done already). How proud she would feel. The distraction rendered her useless at the lunch, with James and Julian being so glamorous themselves. She was star-spotting and willing herself to be starstruck by someone famous soon. What's the use of coming to this amazing place and not see-ing anyone.

"What do you think, Emilee?" nudged Edna.

"Well…" she stalled as Edna jumped in.

"I think logistically, the easiest one to pull off is the Shoreditch venue. The poolside denotes Ibiza perfectly."

"Well, if I could just say, the actual Ibiza venue is more authentic, rather than create a theme…I, think?" redeemed Emilee.

"Yes, we would prefer that too, wouldn't we, Julian?"

"I couldn't agree with you more. We have to bear in mind all the people we expect to turn up at the event will have to fly out. And when the guests become aware that we'll be filming it for telly, there'll be some crucial no-shows and we can't afford that."

"Can you share what the storyline is going to be for this one?" asked Julian trying to garner as much plot as possible.

"Oooh, yes go on Edna. Dare you?" teased James.

"You should know better than to ask you rascals…" she chuckled.

Flat white coffees rounded off the lunch, then the dynamic duo prepared to rush off.

"Stay, order a drink on us. We'll take care of it."

Two pink gin cocktails came after they had signed off the bill.

"Rude not to eh? Cheers Emilee."

"Cheers! Thanks."

"So how have you been finding it with us?" enquired Edna.

"Oh, it's hard, hard work, but I am loving every minute of it," gushed Emilee.

"Has anyone been giving you a hard time or anything? That can happen, so I hope you feel that you can always confide in me."

"Not yet…hahaha…so far, that is."

"I don't just mean the production staff, but the talent as well. Don't let them befriend you or bribe you into anything. It will always compromise your position with the company. Something they don't teach you on media courses."

"Does that happen, then?"

"Of course it does. And it's easily done too. Just be careful and know which side of the cameras you want to be."

"Right. I'm going to ask you something. Just listen to me first before you say anything."

"Oh, sounds ominous."

Emilee became increasingly apprehensive in a paranoid way.

"I have a hunch. Just a hunch mind, that all in The Housewives of House camp is not rosy. They've closed ranks on me, which is quite understandable given what happened to Dande. We had planted the 'bump in' between Dande and Sugar St Jean to unfold in some sort of incident. At least that was the intention. What happened between Piper and Dande threw us completely. We replayed the drama in the viewing suite repeatedly and we can't understand how we never saw it coming. Me in particular. I had spent so much time getting to know them in their habitat and never picked up on any underlying tension."

"You can't be blamed for that."

"Somehow I did miss it. I have been searching for a motive ever since. I never wanted to lose Dande, that's between you and me, but had I spotted this we could have worked with it."

"What are you asking me?"

"Experience has taught me that when the

cameras stop rolling, the real story is revealed behind the scenes, off camera, to the cleaners, hospitality staff and our runners and interns. So, this is where you come in. Cast your mind back. Do you recall hearing anything, or did you notice anything… anything at all that could perhaps put some pieces of this puzzle together?"

"Like…?"

Biding, her time Emilee loosened the waistband at the back of her granite denim jeggings. Should she gamble and say something?

Her head began to itch furiously with nerves. Would there ever be a right time to mention it. If the team did get to the bottom of things and her story was integral to it, she would never be able to claim she knew anything.

"Come on Emilee what're you thinking? I can tell you have something. I promise, anything you say is in confidence and won't affect your job."

Edna cracked that toothy smile of hers as she sipped the gin from her fishbowl glass.

"Can I come and sit there?" asked Emilee pointed to the seat next to Edna. "I need to be a little bit closer for this."

"Yes, yes, sit here!"

Edna's voice had raised three octaves higher in anticipation.

Emilee snuggled in the banquette seat, hugging her drink with both palms, running her tongue against her front teeth.

"The thing is Edna. I did catch something the other day when James and Julian and the crew came to the office. Can't recall which one of the meetings, but we were talking about the wedding ideas and whether the DJs should wear a tux or something like that."

"Yeah, I remember that. Didn't Piper rush off from that meeting? Right in the bloody middle of it? Rude!"

"Gosh your memory's good. They've been in so many times all the meetings have blended into one."

"Ems, spit it out."

"Remember, when I ran out after her? I didn't know where she'd got to. But I could hear her. She was talking on the phone to someone. She sounded distressed. Almost hysterical. It was like she was whispering and then shouting so I couldn't pick up what she was saying exactly."

"What was she saying?"

"Not sure if I've got this right. She said 'you can't let this happen. I love you. I will leave Charlie if I have to'."

Emilee started nodding profusely as if to validate the hearsay as fact.

"Say that again?"

The pair nit and picked every nuance and millisecond of the story together. They made a great team. Emilee was learning from the master. Edna sat back and made her conclusions almost another hour later after the lunch had ended.

"She is having an affair. You don't threaten to leave your husband for cupcakes! What's more she is having an affair with Dande's groom, Eli. What else is the motive for falling out so spectacularly with her best friend? Thing is, I don't think Dande knows. Not sure she even suspects."

Mouth aghast, Emilee was in wide-eyed disbelief.

"How do you make that out?"

"Dande? You've seen her? Heard her? If she knew, Armageddon would break out. No, Dande does not know. It's more likely that she's intuitively picking up a negative vibe from her so-called mate."

"Really?"

"It makes complete sense. On the playback we heard Dande accuse her of hiding her mobile and generally being sneaky around her. She was paranoid that we were working with Piper for the 'bump in'. But we know that not to be the case. We have never colluded with her. I don't know her that well. So what else could Dande be paranoid about...unless Piper is having an affair and hiding it."

"What if she could be having an affair with another family member?"

"Sounded like someone closer. Only someone involved in the group has the power to 'stop the event happening'."

"This is heartbreaking, but I don't see how you can be so sure. I was really nervous about saying anything."

"I had an inkling you had something, didn't I? I was right, wasn't I? Say nothing to anyone. Even Charlotte or Polly, Dorrit, anybody. Even after I've spoken to them. You tell them, I can't talk unless Edna's here. Okay?"

"We have got ourselves one hell of a finale! Whoop!"

Edna realised that response was inappropriate for BAFTA, but, nonetheless, triumphantly led Emilee by the hand towards Jermyn St, to catch a cab.

Despite minor misgivings, Emilee began to feel valued. Edna Wright knew the telly game more than anyone. She had to trust her. A second contract was within touching distance.

A Family Affair

The Stefano family sat together at the table, playing with their helping of overcooked, lamb tagine. Dande had experimented with dates that sweetened the juices into a gloopy syrup.

"Right, Bert, Lola, your mum and me have an announcement to make. We're thinking about getting married."

"Yay! Mummy, Daddy…Mummy can I be a brides-maid? Please…please.."

Lola ran over to hug Dande.

"Hmmm…s'alright, I 'spose," grunted Bertie non-plused.

"I know it's a shock, but we are a family and it has to be a family decision."

"Yeah, right. You don't give a damn what I think. Stop pretending like you care."

"Oi, mate…what's up with you lately? Why you being like this?"

"Bertie, darling, what's wrong?" joined in Dande.

"I'm just saying 'do what you like'. You always do anyway. I've finished eating. I'm going up to my room, if that's okay?"

With that Bertie stormed off while Lola danced and twirled at the news in her princess-bridesmaid-to-be world.

Eli jumped up after him, but Dande managed to

stop him running after him.

"See, this is what he's like most of the time these days. I know he's a teenager, but what do we do?" asked Dande.

"I thought we were going to be the cool parents, but I'm struggling here."

"Listen babe, sit down. Let's do it tonight...let's make out you've got a last-minute gig come in. Pack an overnight bag so that Bertie believes you're off. Order a cab but jump out and sit and wait in the Range. As soon as you've gone it usually takes him half an hour before he just runs out of the house. I'll leave right behind him, jump in the car with you and we can follow him. See where he goes."

"Not this idea again?"

"You got a better one?"

Eli was desperate.

"Let's get it done. We have a wedding coming up and we need the family together. It can't hurt."

"What about Lola?"

"We'll take her with us, it's too late for a babysitter."

"No you won't do that. Leave it with me. I'll just follow him. Keep it simple."

"Okay, but be careful, then, and do it properly. If he's in any trouble tell me before you do anything. Promise me?"

"He's my kid. I've got his best interest at heart. Leave it with me. Trust me...okay?"

"I do trust you. It's a crazy idea, but what else can we do?"

The couple set about with their mock "oh, no, you got a last minute gig...whatabout family time?" row for Bertie's benefit. Hoping he could hear them despite the headphones, so they over egged it a little, but the plan worked.

This was not what Eli had in mind for his evening off. He had the wedding and Piper on his case, but his son had to be his main priority for once.

* * * * *

Eli followed Bertie onto the train. Keeping his distance (and keeping up with him) from separate carriages was tricky. When they got off in Camden he walked up the road, trying to keep up the pace with his athletic son without being seen. Very soon it became apparent that Bertie was heading to the climbing clematis front porch of Claudia Flint-Dunn, his ex-actress grandmother.

Eli's heart was beating faster than it had in a while after the hasty walk. He could hear his breath as he paused to look on. He couldn't see who answered the door, but just that his boy went inside without hesitation. How did Bertie come to know where his grandmother lived? The last time he visited he was only three. Eli was raking the puzzle through his head.

Claudia used to visit or they had the odd meal out together, but it was a rare occasion and not enough for Bertie to form a bond. Eli waited. Waited and waited, but Bertie looked set to stay over. All Eli wanted to do was knock on the door and get to the bottom of it. But as Dande had stressed, the boy's trust and privacy was vital to keeping their relationship as a parent intact. The surest way of building that back up was to let Bertie tell them. Eli jumped in a cab after an hour and a half and headed back home.

"Tell me everything, Eli. What do you think it's all

about?" probed Dande, frustratingly.

"I'm damned if I know. I mean, do you think Amy is behind this?"

"Well, she is his biological mother and it's been at the back of my mind for a while, but just can't see how? Claudia has nothing to do with her anymore."

"Biological? Babe, no offence. You're his mum, but Amy is his mum too. When you put it like that it's not nice."

"Amy Dunn! I swear if I hear her name again in this house. Please don't defend her. She's a crack-head and a junky who gave up her kid."

"Look we all have our problems, but let's not turn this into a row about her. She's still my ex. I love you, we're getting married. She's in the past. But! She's a human being who's had a bad lot. We all take drugs..."

"I'm not shouting...I'm just saying she has been a cloud hanging over us forever and poor Bertie must pick up on it. Maybe that's it."

"Nobody likes to hear bad things said about their mother. Your one is a fucking pain to you, but I'm not allowed to say anything."

Silence.

"...ah, see?"

Dande would have launched into a seething row at this juncture, but wedding fever was never far away, a calming reminder of the positives to come.

"Babe, all I can tell you is he will be back in the morning. Claudia will take care of him. He either goes straight to school or comes barging in up to his room."

"I hated leaving him there. Not knowing what he's up to, though. Wish you had told me about all this before."

"Eli...please don't blame me. I'm doing my best."

"I'll get to the bottom of this in the morning, if I have to drag him out of school to do it. This behaviour is not on."

This stance taken by Eli was that of a balanced and authoritative father figure, a side Dande rarely saw in him. He was actually beginning to look like husband material at last.

*****

It had been a difficult night. Neither Dande or Eli slept well, worrying about Bertie. Then at last the sound of keys in the door.

"Here he comes," said Dande, gesturing to Eli. "The prodigal son. He'll lock himself in his room for a while then come down for snacks...if he smells warmed up pain au chocolat from the oven, he'll be down quicker still."

"What is he? Some trained rabbit or something. Is this what you've been doing with him?"

Eli's accusatory slant was not going down well with her.

"Why are you criticising me? All I have ever done is provided a routine and comforts for our children. The way we live is already arse over backwards. So no, it's not magic tricks, it's learning what makes them happy and providing it. What the fuck would you even know...you're hardly ever here!" snapped Dande.

"I didn't mean anything...calm down, will you?"

"Do you want one, then?"

Dande counted out the pre-baked goods from the freezer.

"Yeah, I'll have two of those. Erm, thank you."

Brewing the coffee on the stove the way Eli liked

it was going to be a giveaway that he was home, so
Dande explained this and stalled the process.

"Okay, he's coming...don't attack him..." she
whispered.

"Oh? Dad?"

Bertie stopped in his tracks at the kitchen
entrance.

Dande raised her eyebrows and put on the coffee.

"Where were you last night, son?"

"Where were you?" retaliated Bertie.

"Don't get cheeky. It's a simple question. So?"

"I don't know what you get up to away from here.
Why do I have to tell you anything?"

"Are we doing this Bertram? Really? I'm your
father, so don't talk to me like that. How did we get
here, mate?"

"Boring..."

"Excuse me? Okay. I know where you were, I followed you."

"Oh no, Eli..."

Dande was disappointed at Eli's tactics.

"You followed me...you were playing out?"

"I lied."

"I don't get it. Followed me where?"

"I wanted you to tell me yourself rather than this
cat 'n mouse conversation."

"I'm going out...see ya!"

"Oh no you don't..."

Eli grabbed him and sat him down on the
armchair. Bertie knew it was useless to fight his Dad's
strong build.

"I don't want to fight you, son. I love you very
much. Your mum does too. But we are worried about
you. You can't go marching off to God knows where
like this. It's London...anything can happen. Don't

you understand? Tell me why you went to Granny Claudia's?"

"You followed me…for real? I don't believe it! That's fucked up!"

"Watch it!"

"Why are you treating me like a child?"

"Classic. Look, what's she got over there? I'll call her myself."

"No. Don't Dad. Please!"

"Oh my God, is she bullying you? What is it, matey? Come on, I'm not gonna cause you any grief. Trust me. I'm here on your side."

Eli patted his son's back and kissed his forehead.

Bertie began to sob, as Dande tried to put a side plate of pan au chocolat in front of him, as if it would solve anything. He shook his head, refusing her offering.

"I got teased at school on WhatsApp when someone posted a link of Granny Claudia in some lame seventies film. I googled her myself and all this shit came up about her wild child daughter Amy Dunn. That's my fuckin' mother the papers was writing about. They made her out to be slag!"

"Ooooh, mate. Son, listen. I'm sorry I should've sat you down and told you about this stuff. It should've come from me. I'm gutted you dealt with this on your own."

"Bert, don't believe everything you read. Your mum was a beautiful young woman, you know."

Dande never thought she'd say any of that.

"Well, she isn't anymore…" sobbed Bertie, starting to cry profusely.

It terrified his parents to see him like this.

"They both kneeled down in front of him eager to comfort him until he was ready to talk. They didn't want to embarrass him and yet leave him enough space. Dande pulled one more trick out of the bag and offered to make him his favourite chocolate milkshake with banana flavoured cream topping. The double choc was his go-to comfort food. He sat up on the kitchen island, sniffing and eating. Then they spoke again.

"So how is Granny Claudia? Is she nice to you?"

"Yes, she is really kind."

"Are we talking about the same person? She hated me. I was always sneezing in front of her. She thought I was full of germs, but it was that stinking perfume of hers I was allergic to. Does she still…"

"Yes! Haha…I sneeze as well. The whole house stinks of it!"

The mood was lifting. Once Dande had spotted the breakthrough she left father and son to confide. In the meantime, she hid and listened at the door.

Bertie wanted to find his mum and thought that his Granny Claudia would help him. She didn't at first, but one day he paid her a visit and a blonde lady was there. She was bubbly and full of personality when his Granny introduced him to his estranged mother. Amy received her son with open arms. She hugged him, kissed him and apologised for abandoning him. She told him that she loved him and that he must stay in touch, but to never tell Eli or Dande.

Bertie said he felt obliged to follow the one favour his mum had asked of him. He also noticed that Eli and Dande argued about Amy Dunn all the time. But she was his mum and he never knew the real story of why he was left to grow up with his dad. However, the next time he would meet his mum there, she was 'different', her hair was lank, her eyes sunken and she barely spoke. When she did it was a croaky child-like wailing. It creeped him out and he was too shocked to take it in and ran out of the house.

Eli pushed his son to tell him more. He wanted all of it in order to help his son push forward. Bertie told how angry he was and still is after seeing his mum like that. Barely moving, no eye contact.

He got more and more confused because each time he saw his mum she was in a different state. She wasn't always there on every visit, but mostly. The worst came when he heard his Granny crying on the phone. Amy had been sectioned again and wasn't going to be at Granny's for a while. He didn't really know what mental health was about until a school project, which he stopped attending. He couldn't come to terms with finding her and realising she wasn't herself. He wanted to know which was the real her. Would he ever know? However, he still wanted to see Granny Claudia hoping she would take him to visit his mother, but she refused and "will never set foot in a place like that, never."

At every twist and turn of his son's outpouring Eli hugged him and kissed him.

"Don't worry," he whispered, hugging him. "I love you, boy."

Dande wiped tears from her face, blaming herself that the poor lad had to deal with this alone. She had joined Al Anon to help.

Eli then made a solemn pledge that he would take him to visit his mum at the hospital and invite Granny Claudia over more often.

He shouted Dande to join him in the pledge that they would never argue about Amy Dunn again and whatever he needed to know he had just to ask.

They also promised that they would talk about his mum and tell stories of how she used to be before she had addictions.

Dande looked over to one of her Buddha statues and bowed, "Namaste". Thankful for Christopher's advice, she must invite him and his wife to the wedding, she told herself.

Spending quality time with his son from then on resulted in Bertie's bad attitude dissipating very quickly. Back at school and more involved with the family, especially with the wedding coming up. There were no shortages of Eli's special hugs for Dande. As a couple they had never been stronger. As a family they were indestructible.

Welcome To The Jungle

It had been a long slog for the production team, but nonetheless an exciting one, developing a new concept, combining self-contained episodes under-pinned by a thin veil of an arc leading to an explosive finale, unique in its coverage of the talent involved.

The superstar DJ is big news, but what of the wives and girlfriends? Capturing them living the party lifestyle and bringing up kids.

The key production team members had a few days sitting in the edits browsing through rushes of what they had covered so far. Were they meeting the brief set out by the channel? How glamorous was the wow factor and how appealing would it be to the now middle-aged rave generation.

So far they had shot Suki Chung and DJ Razr Denzle hosting dinner for The Housewives of House and their DJ partners in their minimalist Maida Vale home; Clara Molehill at her Kensal Rise home, a party house, talking to Nancy about her IVF treatments; Nancy and Suki walking little Kitty to the Montessori after coffee in her Queens Park garden flat.

Piper featured heavily in the series. They shot her at home exploring her walk-in closet after a staged shopping trip in Bond Street. The housewives all came back while she tried on her purchases; they went vintage clothes shopping in Portobello Road, coffees and drinks in Kensal Rise; taking their SUVs to the car shop for repairs and test driving new ones; nail bars and hair salons also in Portobello; an Ibiza Magazine launch; festival launch, press night; seafood in Notting Hill Gate; a street art gallery exhibition; supper club nights.

The name-dropping had become a problem, The Housewives of House were connected to far too many established creatives to get clearances from. The named pop-stars, racing drivers, sporting personalities, interior designers, art directors, journalists, MPs, artists and even TV producers resided somewhere in the Kensal Triangle neighbour- hood and were a part of their daily life.

They were either friends or the friends of, or making new friends over giant glasses of wine at home, usually with at least one caner present lead- ing them astray. A respectable lifestyle with families in the home counties, cottage and villa rentals, pri- vate healthcare and faux left-leaning values.

The conversations of 21st Century chattering classes follow a set pattern up and down the country. Ritualistic in their endeavours, but unlike every other tribe, they get to go about their lives hidden in plain sight. Inoffensive portrayals in the media of them- selves by themselves. This show was playing with fire on the verge of dispelling the 'lifestyle' myth.

The accepted understanding of the after-dinner etiquette, where one deserts the desserts to continue the deep one-to-one chat away from the others over a scoop of the white stuff to clarify one's point further. Overlooked, is the glaring intimacy of this privacy, snorting in close proximity human to human. A general acceptance, careful not to misconstrue that this connection means anything more. Until of course, it does.

Directing the 'bump in' element of constructed drama for reality TV had become an art form by now. This first series was about getting to know the talent and bumping into each other was a reduced element of surprise. The finale would have to bring about the drama as a cliffhanger into the next series. A carefully-guarded secret.

They wanted to see informative, comedic and pathos-led episodes into an evenly balanced format that would capture the zeitgeist of 'party people parents'. A west London hub where the ladies that 'raunched', had a post Sunday lunch buzz or a cheeky mid-week sit-up. Their stories, as yet untold, carried commercial responsibilities.

* * * * *

"We're almost all set for the finale. The tension brewing up nicely between Piper and Dande. Wink-wink," mumbled Charlotte in the latest production meeting. "Roll on showtime…"

Edna had misgivings. She was apprehensive about meddling with something as sacred as tying nuptials. It seemed a bridge too far. It wasn't that she was losing her edge, it was more that she was lonely herself. Still searching for the one, and with no time for a romantic connection she was beginning to empathise with Dande. This attitude would not bode well for career longevity in this genre.

* * * * *

"I thought you were the one who had the big

dreams...all those dance lessons and drama school fees? For what?"

Mrs Lyon was indignant.

"I loved it, but never got my chance," replied Dande ruefully. "And I just don't want to teach dancing."

"Teaching is a respectable job. You could have a good career in that, like your sister."

"I am not my sister."

"Tch! I know. But you throw away your opportunity for a man who plays records? He can't do that forever! Who is he? What else can he do?"

"It's my life to throw away, mama. I'll throw it where I want. Since Lola was born you have nagged for me to get married and here I am, about to, and it's still not enough."

Dande looked at Mrs L scornfully as she shuffled and mumbled in French, before adding: "I can't believe you're allowing them to organise the happiest day of your life?"

"Mother, please. Let me tell you what else they're doing..."

Dande was trying not to get riled up.

"You invited your father?"

"For the last time, yes. I have. You can bring your plus one."

"I don't have one."

"I know you do, whatsisname? Err..."

"Leave him out of it. He prunes my roses and my garden is so nice now."

"I'll bet...anyhoo, he is welcome but I have to get numbers in a.s.a.p."

"So what about the cake? Your sister could have made you one if you spoke to her."

"It has to be a professional one. They've got it

covered and it is gorgeous!!!"

"What about all the cars to take us up there?"

"Done."

"They haven't left me anything to do…"

"I know…isn't that great, Mum?"

"Hmmpf …!"

Mrs Lyon was put out that her daughter never understood her role as her mother. She had made one mistake. The Anglo/French mother left her daughters alone with their French/Caribbean father for one year. Abandoned them without explanation and returned out of the blue and moved back in the family home. Her Dad became nervous that she would leave them again. He was hurt for the girls who he could not console or didn't understand. They split up again when the girls were in their twenties, but the damage had been done. The sisters never spoke.

"Your main job mum will be to take care of Lola. There'll be too many people about so watch her, her welfare is what will worry me most on the day."

"You should worry about your fiancé. Hope he turns up. Hmmpf…"

"Mum? Why do you have to be like this?"

"Like what?"

"Dad will be walking me down the aisle. Eli will be my Prince Charming. Bertie will be the handsomest best man and Lola the prettiest flower girl…you should see her dress!"

"Why can't you show me anything?"

"I told you, the TV people need to keep these things a secret until the show is aired. I've signed an agreement not to tell, otherwise I would."

"You always do things different to my taste. Hmmpf."

"Mum are you happy for me? Look at my ring?"

"It's nice."

"I'm not gonna fall out with you Mum. Try and act a little bit more enthusiastic for me. That's all. You're getting a designer suit as mother-of-the-bride."

"I don't know about the colour...navy isn't my colour."

"Think about how fat Eli's mum is going to look in the lemon!"

"Like a pat of butter...ha!"

"Hahaha...Mum, it's almost all done. The hotel is being dressed with loads of green foliage and palms by the pool. Downstairs the ceremony room is all white, with white rocks and white flowers. The food looks fantastic with silver service. Very classy, Mum. All the party guests will arrive for the wedding supper by the pool! There'll be loads of faces too. Not sure you'll recognise them, but it's going to be the best thing ever! I'm so happy. I feel so lucky!"

"Sounding very grand. You always like the flash life. But Dande Lyon, after the way they treated you with the first show, I don't trust them. I just don't."

"Everybody is saying that, but they wouldn't go to this expense. They have been nothing but super nice to me. Anything I want they get. They're eager to please me. Everyone deserves a second chance. People make mistakes, don't they?"

Dande was on dangerous territory inferring her mother was given a second chance. It was time to leave.

"Bye mum, I'll come over again next week!"

Wed-ding Dong

The night before the wedding, the swanky private members hotel was spilling over with close family and production crew, props and florists, joiners and electricians. All The Housewives of House had a room each, but the action was naturally scheduled to be filmed in Dande's room...when she was in her bridal gown, on the day only. Another small snippet was to be shot on the wedding morning, but they had to 'cheat it' so it appeared to be the day before. It all seemed a bit hush hush, but in a good way.

Piper was distraught about Eli going through with it. She felt bitter about his rejection and tormented herself about the whole filming set up. Would it go according to the producers' plans and how would she feel if something went wrong? She had not discussed what was to come with anyone...except Charlie, of course.

*****

"There's a cocktail bar on the other floor, let's head down there," ushered Eli.

Holding a sangria each, they supped on the Spanish national drink.

"Congratulations, fella. No pulling out now," gushed Charlie.

"I was trying not to drink beforehand, but failing miserably...thanks, mate."

"How do you think Dande is taking to all this?"

"She is in her element, actually. We've been good for a while now...you know, ups and downs. Bertie was a major factor, but he's finally coming around. All is good in the Stefano household, thanks."

"Cheers..."

Charlie paused and then spoke.

"So would you turn down a 10k gig?"

"Whooah! No way. You got one?"

"Yeah I couldn't turn it down."

"So what's the deal?"

"It's tomorrow."

"But that's the...?"

"Wedding, I know..."

"So why the hell...nope, do it mate. I would. It's in the evening, right?"

"That's the bad bit...listen...and please, if I tell you this you cannot breathe a word. It will fuck so many things up. But you're my mate, hope you'd do the same for me."

"What Fenners?"

"Look, I'll be able to make the first part of the wedding and the speeches, but not the evening party...sorry mate. I've been asked to play at DJ Jesmond Harrison's secret engagement supper in Mayfair."

"You are joking? Tell me this is a wind up."

Eli placed his drink on the bar and does a deliberate 360 turn on the spot.

"I only got told about this, Thursday. It's a secret so obviously..."

"So we're likely to lose some of our guests to his?" asked Eli through gritted teeth.

"You're not wrong there, but it sounds like an intimate thing."

"Jeez, he's not engaged to that trollop is he?"

"Sugar? 'Fraid so!"

"Whatabout Piper?"

"She's coming with me. We're both invited as guests and ..." winced Charlie "...it's being filmed... tch!"

"Filmed? By this lot???"

Charlie nodded.

"The mother freakin' fuckers...fuck, fuck, fuck! Two faced bastards."

Eli was so fiercely angry, Charlie was terrified he had blown everything. He placed two hands on his shoulders trying to calm him down. Averting any attention from the bar staff.

"Eli, Eli, wait, wait...it shouldn't be a problem, because by the time Dande gets wind of it, you'll be wed and she'll probably not notice we've left. Her and Piper are properly distant these days...so it might just pan out?"

"You're so naïve, Charlie," fumed Eli, belting down the bar to the lifts. "See ya tomorrow, yeah."

Had he just made an error of epic proportions, wondered Charlie.

Piper would kill him, also for ruining the dramatic 'bump in'. He didn't think it was fair on Dande. But who could refuse £10k for a night's work? He considered whether an extra special wedding pressie would help. He was terrified of telling Piper what he had done.

*****

Eli ran out of the lift to the main door, pushing the

wedding staff out of the way. Marching down the street he looked for the nearest coffee shop of which there were multiples from which to choose in Shoreditch. The one with the darkest corners seemed apt. He had one call to make.

"Eli…"

Piper had let it ring until she found an escape route to hide, overjoyed to hear from him at last.

He must have come to his senses or was getting cold feet, she assumed. Maybe he just wanted her one last time. She didn't care. He had called her. For a moment it was the best feeling she had in a long time.

"I don't care who you're with, what you're doing or where you are, but you better find yourself here now. I'm at The Colombian Brew across the road."

Then he hung up.

Agitated with trepidation of Eli's angry tone, Piper lifted her maxi dress for faster movement. One minute she was cup half full, he loved her after all, then cup half empty.

*****

He saw her approaching through the glass window, intercepted her entrance and grabbed her by the hand so her maxi dress tripped her up as he frog-marched her to a graffiti wall off the main drag.

"What are you doing? Let me go!" Piper cried out in abject horror at his anger.

"Just tell me. Tell me what the score is!"

"Score?"

"The fucking film cunts…are you setting us up? Dande and me? Is this some scorned shit for you?"

"Holy crap…what are you on about? You're fucking crazy. You know what, Dande is welcome to you."

"I know everything - about Jesmond's not so fuck-ing secret engagement!"

"I don't know what you're talking about. I don't know."

"Do me a favour, spare the lies. Tell me!"

"No, no idea what you're on about."

Piper glared at him and held her fury hanging by her water filled eyes.

"Ok. I get it. Tell you what, let's go on with the show, shall we? See where it gets us. You fuck about with Dande's day and I promise, I will make you pay. Believe me. Now fuck off. I hate to even look at you."

Eli strutted off.

Piper was sobbing against the wall. The way he looked at her with disdain, a hurt so final when love has died...it was over between them, for good this time.

Apathy ensued her listless mind and body as she shuffled back to the hotel. She was going to need more gear than she had with her to see her through the next 24 hours. Clara might have an extra gram, but she needed to call her dealer and load up fast.

Back among the production crew fussing, it was noticeable that the light had gone out of Piper's eyes. She sniffled heavily and put it down to a cold, but her sudden urge to cry every few minutes could not be suppressed.

Suki embraced her.

"You're such a softie...we're all sobbing as well."

Piper held that thought as her excuse to explain her red eyes. She tried to get some alone time, but Charlie was there, avoiding eye contact, rallying around the kids, the TV and ordering pizzas in the room.

Piper locked herself in the hotel ensuite bathroom for a long soak. She just wanted to slip away from the world. A world not worth living in without Eli.

He had more or less threatened her. Was there any one thing she could do to halt the wedding, she floundered for even thinking it. She would counter-threaten him by instructing her new agent and lawyer. She could plead that she only acted under contractual obligations. He would never risk admitting to their affair. Dande would never forgive him. On the upside he would be a single man again. She lay quiet, still in the bath, haunted by her predicament. She tried to remind herself why she had agreed to go to the secret engagement supper, on the day her best friend was tying the knot. The more she thought about it, she realised Dande would be the most hurt by it and her anger wasn't aimed at her. It was at Eli. How much had she let the sisterhood down by becoming involved with this man? He was no good for Dande, nor herself. She was no fan of Sugar St Jean, but with two events to feign interest in on the same day would qualify her for a BA first in a study of insincerity.

How had Eli found out? DJs were the worst gossips, claiming bragging rights worthy of any champion heavyweight boxer. DJ Jesmond Harrison was surrounded by them.

Despite going to bed early, she lay awake through the night, welcoming the 5.30am call time. She had been racking up gear non-stop, and planned on chain-coking the next 24 hours, at least. This was to be a day where she would be channeling the fresh wounds of a dream shattered. No amount of makeup and styling would disguise that fact.

*****

There was much prep for the first scene, cheating the pre-wedding meet to include Dande. Piper was directed to break the news of Sugar St Jean's invitation after the actual wedding vows had been done. This way Dande still had her dream wedding until The Housewives of House reached its climactic finale.

Dande's reaction was unpredictable, but they knew there would be one. The tension between her and the Maid of Honour would be reignited in their gorgeous gowns. Piper was rethinking these plans, with the intention of revealing the truth sooner than outlined, which might prevent the wedding from occurring in the first place. She didn't know whether she had it in her to be that brave. Was it too cruel? She was going to leave it to impulse.

The setting was the rooftop corner away from the pool with the City of London views in the background. The Housewives of House were styled in colour bloc, for a sophisticated nod to a hen lunch. They had to make out it was the day before the wedding. How they struggled to keep up the pretence. They huddled together beaming and loving life in Diane Von Furstenberg, Roland Mouret, Elie Saab and McQueen. Sofia Sieben hadn't done too a shabby a job. Reena would have approved.

"I can't wait to see Dande's dress. What's it like, Piper?" asked Nancy.

"All will be revealed tomorrow. She'll look so special on the day."

"You can tell us about your dress, though?" added Suki.

"I have a couple of options to choose from, believe it or not. I have an Alice Temperley or a Vera Wang… they are both stunning. I feel like royalty in them."

"Ah, here she comes, the beautiful Bride-To-Be!" Clara cried out and the first to "mwah" the 5'10" formidable, statuesque figure in a silk tangerine catsuit.

"How do you do it, Glamazon!"

Nancy was next.

"Thank you, ladies. Thanks for making the effort, you all look gorgeous as well. Save something for tomorrow…mwah!"

"Are you very nervous darling?" continued Nancy.

"Yes, I can't believe it is happening after so long. My wedding planners James and Julian have been amazing so far…am I a lucky girl or what?"

"Have you seen Eli yet?" wondered Suki.

"Yes, he's as nervous as I am. So sweet."

"So glad we get to be a part of your big day," assured Clara.

"Well said…ahem. As your Maid of Honour, let's raise a toast to the bride-to-be, thank you for choosing me. I love you and wish you all the best wishes in the world. May all your wine glasses be lead crystal and stay filled with love and happiness!" Piper had rehearsed these lines well. Almost sincere. They joined in a lively rendition of the house classic Love and Happiness by Masters At Work ft Indya. Clara trying to beatbox ended the segue on a high.

* * * * *

Piper had bottled it. There was going to be a wedding after all.

The production team and film crew were all po-faced and switched to 'on', radio headsets and call sheets in hand. There was only one chance to capture the whole event. There wasn't going to be a re-shoot. Their adrenaline swept over the room.

For the sake of privacy, ironically, the production company was restricted to shooting scenes of the bride's entrance only...and leave before the exchange of vows. Then they would be allowed to return when the couple walked down the aisle as Mr & Mrs Lyon-Stefano.

The white room's flooring sparkled with white astro turf. The walls were covered in white rose buds and giant glass rocks. The silk canopy ceiling with white and silver Moroccan lanterns spread warm led lights.

There were three harpists that created the most ethereal sound.

Lola, Poppy and Kitty and Eli's twin nieces were ringleted, flower girls in white ballerina tutus and slippers. With the exception of the almost four-year-old Poppy, each carried a basket containing spiritual symbols, feathers, white petals, blue petals and sprinkles of ground rose quartz.

The Humanist ceremony was nondescript. The registrar was a skinny, black woman who went OTT in a white cocktail gown for herself.

The Housewives of House were resplendent in the second row, Clara in vintage Dolce & Gabbana, Nancy in Lanvin and Suki in Azzedine Alaïa. Refusing to walk down the aisle with the plausible excuse of "not wishing to take anything away from Dande's special moment", Piper opted for the Temperley dress, taking her place in the front row. It was enough that she had already been styled to outdo the bride in the unashamedly glamorous, powder blue frock. No one had picked up the frosty manner between her and Eli. There was no polite handshake or kiss greeting and they avoided direct eye contact. His knee shook, he was worried sick about what Piper might do.

He glanced Mrs Lyon from the corner of his eyes in her navy skirt suit and red poppy hat, who was in easy reach to tear him limb from limb with her bare hands if anything was to go wrong.

James and Julian Moran, who caustically made their perfectionist presence felt just hours earlier, casually sauntered in their signature look, sporting blue and purple suits, swapped colour jackets.

Once seated, they gave the nod and the hush came over the room as the harpists plucked the intro to Sade's Cherish The Day and from beyond the decor a female soprano sang out 'You're ruling the way that I move…' by the time she sang the words 'won't catch me running' that was the cue. The little ballerina flower girls stumbled out bringing tears to their mothers' eyes, sprinkling the various symbols from their baskets and nothing like the way they had rehearsed it.

The wedding singer sang out 'You show me how deep love can be' as the harps plucked bass notes precipitating waves of emotion over the guests. Escorted by her towering 6'4 father in his silk cobalt blue Oswald suit, all eyes were laid on her as she made a demure entrance. Magnificent, in a Gautier wedding dress Dande got her 'wow' moment.

The intricate silks and lace that drew the eyes up and down and accented her figure was spellbinding. The design captured the bohemian, vintage vision Dande had in mind. The detailed finish with its open keyhole at the back was the perfect focal point as the vows were exchanged. Eli's pursed lip expression was fixed as anxiety got the better of him. Overwhelmed by this angelic beauty coming towards him, who could have anyone, but had chosen to marry him of all people, had him choked. Rescued by his best man, Bertram giving him a gentle reassuring pat on the back.

The celebrations kicked off as their exit music Around by Noir & Haze with its sub bass line, an Ibiza anthem for the couple a few years before. The party heads cheered as they took over fist pumping and hollering to the chorus 'get ya, get ya!' Not forgetting the all-important air piano riff of this tune.

The cameras were on and the production crew's floodlights splashed the tinsel.

*****

Wedding breakfast served, speeches made, cake cut, the lull that followed before the evening guests arrived where the Ibiza themed poolside was taking shape. The staff in Hawaiian shirts serving cocktails and the DJs in the house getting the groove on with their Balearic warm ups...

The bride and groom were scurried away from their guests to a staged backdrop of palm trees to take press and publicity photos. They took ages; Cater Moran Events needed some, as did the production company as did the PR and marketing for TV listings, etc. The forty or so minutes was beginning to drag on. Eli wrestled uncomfortably because Piper was due at some point to drop the bomb. He racked his mind for how he could restrain Dande's outburst or for what method had worked before.

He did not recognise that some of the DSLR cameras shoot video these days. The whole posing for pictures was already being recorded and tested for sound.

"Emilee, get the Maid of Honour, quickly. In fact,

gather the rest of the girls...these will be lovely..." demanded Charlotte.

"Oh, come on, can we give it a rest? You must have all the pictures you need by now. We've been here ages," sighed Eli.

"Just one with all the girls Eli, sorry."

"We've done those already..."

"It's alright, Eli..."

Dande seized her opportunity to milk the spot-light.

"Right, here they are. Guys, let's have one with just Piper and Dande. Can makeup touch up the others please."

"You two, sit together, arm linking arm...that's it. Now chatter away naturally."

"Piper, it's been such a good day and the party is gonna be on point! I can tell already! I'm officially Mrs Lyon-Stefano!"

"Ah, about the party," came Piper's intrepid response. "Charlie's got an important gig...we both have to leave early. Sorry."

"More important than my wedding? You have to be kidding me?"

"No it's not more important, but Charlie is obli-gated."

"What the fuck, Pi?"

Eli looked on, squirming. He didn't want to be on camera, but instead did a warning scowl at Piper. Charlie was nowhere to be seen.

"I know, I'm sorry, hun."

"Where is it or what is it, perhaps we can tell them ..."

Before she could finish Piper dived in.

"It's a secret engagement supper in Mayfair."

"Whose engagement?"

The Housewives of House started to sense the trouble brewing from the stark body language and the slightly raised voices.

"Brace yourself, it's for Jesmond Harrison and Sugar St Jean?" admitted Piper.

"Excuse me? Is she for real? Of all the days to pull a stunt like this she's chosen my wedding day?"

Dande's temperament was rising slowly.

"It wasn't up to me?"

"It's never your fault…and breathe…and relax," Dande coaxed herself out loud.

"Nope. I am not gonna rise to this. Georgette Jonsson is pregnant with Jes's baby anyway. Ha. Ha. Ha… it's my wedding day. I'm deliriously happy and that bitch is not gonna ruin it for me. Ohh nooo!"

Suki, Nancy, Clara gathered quickly, picking up the story. Gasping having been kept in the dark themselves. Eli leaned on the console table nearby, shell-shocked she had let the cat out of the bag regarding Jesmond's secret baby. However, if that was her worst reaction…Mrs Dande Lyon-Stefano finally grew up, he thought. What a day.

Charlotte was wondering whether the 'bump in' plan B was going to be necessary. The pre-empted drama fell flat like a cowpat on floor tiles. Despite being compensated with the little baby news aside. Frantic whispers on radio headsets as the production crew flurried on standby for the 'say so'.

Edna froze in concern, praying they wouldn't resort to clumsily outing the Eli/Piper affair. It was out of her control.

"Oh? I'm so glad you've taken it well. Hate falling out with you," exclaimed Piper.

"No worries. I don't want bad energy around the happiest day of my life."

Dande shrugged. Piper shrugged back.

"Eli, have you seen the kids? Sorry guys are we done here?" asserted Dande.

"Yup, we're done," sighed Charlotte. "Talent relax, crew take your positions."

"Let's go have ourselves a party, shall we?" schemed Clara.

"Pardy! Pardy!" clapped Nancy.

The Housewives were off, or so they were led to believe. Charlotte had a hunch and Edna had a hunch about Charlotte's hunch.

Piper was feeling sheepish among her friends, who were bemused by what they just heard. It would keep. Meanwhile, the banter erupted in earnest.

"I cannot believe they have literally turned the rooftop pool into a resort!"

"Aren't they clever?"

"I'm not getting in, though...not in this dress!"

"The bride has got to jump in! And the groom, Eli."

"Hoho, don't know about that. I just hope they don't get chlorine over my speakers."

"Are you playing a set tonight then?"

"Er, yeah. It's my wedding so gonna play my mixes on my bass bins."

"I bet you'd marry the buggers if you could," joked Dande.

Piper anxious to smooth things over, joined in.

"Yeah...the right one, Big Ben with the beer stains is the favourite!"

Eli scowled at her again. She almost forgot her beef with him for a minute.

"How did you get them up here? They're huge!" laughed Clara.

He still frowned.

"Tell you what, I'm weirdly looking forward to seeing them. He never stops going on about them...hahaha."

Dande was on a high.

Pregnant pause.

Suddenly, Piper howled in pain as her hair was yanked violently, twisting her neck.

"How the fuck do you know what his bass bins look like? Bitch! I've been down there a hundred times but I've never been inside that studio, you cow!"

Dande went in for steady grip before anyone could hold her back.

"Tell me, when were you down the studios? Bi-atch!!!"

Then pandemonium broke out as Eli, The House-wives of House, the crew and event staff tried and failed to release Dande's unyielding vice-like hold on Piper's hair.

The heart jolt force of adrenaline pumped through Charlotte as she robotically demanded: "Have you got that? Did you get it?!"

"In the can. Still rolling," a thumbs up confirmed.

Charlotte eyeballed Edna and, with an almighty reverse fist-pump, croaked a triumphant "YES!"

Acknowledgements

Kerry Coburn **Thank you** #kismetencounters
Racquel Milan - My Empress Guide.
Mom & Dad (RIP), Prudence, Winsome, Carole, Glasford, Blair (the apple of my eye...and...wow! Blair...well done!) Josh and Colleen.
My English teachers, Mr Duxbury and Mr Krayer.
Disco, jazz-funk, boogie and house music.
The Masons Arms, The Whippet Inn, North London Tavern, The Salusbury, The Paradise, The Parlour, The Cow, The Westbourne, London, The Cock & Bottle, The Chamberlayne, E&O, The Electric, Pizza East.
Mr Brandon Block – for the book that inspired so many others.
Aine Doris for spurring me on...mwaw!
Thank you:- Lisa O'Meara, Lilamani De Silva, Jane Adams, Ann Smith, Dr Sara Sylvester, Jenny Small, Scorpiane Gayle, Lea Mason.
iPhone X.
Reena Qureshi.
Oprah Winfrey and Vanessa Feltz.
Brenda Emmanus.
The Notting Hill Carnival.
Gilles Peterson.
Paul Trouble Anderson.
Tony Blackburn.
Bulldog and the Birmingham jazz-funk crew.
George Michael.

Aretha Franklin...Respect.

Thanks to the hospitality of the following venues, where I sit, sip and write:

St Helen's Deli, now Adriana's W10
Kitchen & Pantry W11
Portobello Coffee W11
Portobello House W10
Prices Tea Room W11
Cafe Porto W11
St Marks Park W10
The Eagle W10
St Helens Cafe/Bakery W10
The Mall Tavern W11
The Earl of Lonsdale W11

About The Author

Jaqi Loye-Brown is an emerging British author determined to drop novellas derived from her life's interactions into the big pond.

She flatly refuses to be pigeonholed artistically and absolutely rejects cliques. Belonging is overrated. Her stories reflect observations of those on the quest for conformity, status and love.

In and out of the music business, via television and clubland, encounters with a rich glut of creatives have helped shaped her characters and stories, harnessed by a sparklingly, tireless imagination.

Jaqi's leap from singer/spokenword/lyricist to novelist has influenced her writing technique. She explains: "The sensitivity that a musical chord presents empowers the simplest word."

Her maverick approach as a writer is her attempt to sing words off the page, thus a more memorable read, emotive and stirring...even if it's shitstirring.

Also on MT Ink

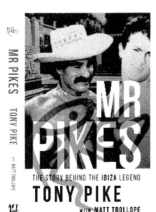

Mr Pikes - The Story Behind The Ibiza Legend - Tony Pike

The playboy who built himself a playground reveals all in his electric memoir.

The iconic hotelier reflects on a life of hedonism and the globe-trotting backstory that influenced his creation of pioneering Balearic boho bolthole, Pikes.

Pike talks candidly about his relationships with hotel guests and friends including George Michael, Freddie Mercury, Julio Iglesias and lover Grace Jones...and also goes exclusively behind the scenes at the Club Tropicana video shoot.

The Life & Lines of Brandon Block

Brandon strips back his dramatic life as we chart the meteoric rise of a cocky schoolboy from Wembley who became an Ibiza legend along the way. A symbol for an acid house generation of excess, Brandon headlined a clubland era that changed the lives of millions.

His spiralling drug habit peaked at an amazing ounce of cocaine a day but somehow he survived to tell the tale. Includes extra chapters published in 2017 as Brandon prepared to enter the Celebrity Big Brother house.

DJ Whore - Jaqi Loye-Brown

In pre-Millennial London Heavenly Angel, the alter-ego of disillusioned Yvonne-Leigh, worships at the altar and ego of DJ Starkey Moran.

Jaqi Loye-Brown's debut DJ Whore is set in the late 1990s, peering over the shoulders of the movers and shakers, fakers and takers.

Through her Portobello Novella series, Jaqi explores the frayed hem of a cutting edge era, tiptoeing through a clubscene rarely explored in a chick-lit.

Printed in Great Britain
by Amazon

18610667R00112